George Morley

In Russet Mantle Clad

Scenes of Rural Life

George Morley

In Russet Mantle Clad
Scenes of Rural Life

ISBN/EAN: 9783337168421

Printed in Europe, USA, Canada, Australia, Japan

Cover: Foto ©Andreas Hilbeck / pixelio.de

More available books at **www.hansebooks.com**

In Russet Mantle Clad

Scenes of Rural Life

BY

GEORGE MORLEY

AUTHOR OF

'LEAFY WARWICKSHIRE,' 'IN RUSTIC LIVERY,' 'SWEET AUDREY,' ETC.

DEDICATED BY SPECIAL PERMISSION TO

THE RIGHT HONOURABLE

The Countess of Warwick

With Illustrations taken specially for this Work

LONDON

SKEFFINGTON & SON, 163 PICCADILLY

Publishers to H.M. The Queen and to H.R.H. The Prince of Wales

1897

' Under the greenwood tree,
  Who loves to lie with me,
  And turn his merry note
  Unto the sweet bird's throat.
Come hither, come hither, come hither ;
        Here shall we see
        No enemy,
But winter and rough weather.'

As You Like It (ACT II., SCENE V.)

DEDICATION

TO

Frances Evelyn Greville,

COUNTESS OF WARWICK,

IN TOKEN OF HER KINDLY FRIENDSHIP,

THESE SCENES OF IDYLLIC LIFE IN WARWICKSHIRE—

THE WORK OF MY HAND WITH MY HEART IN IT

—ARE, BY HER SPECIAL PERMISSION,

VERY GRATEFULLY INSCRIBED.

GEORGE MORLEY

' Howe'er it be it seems to me,
'Tis only noble to be good ;
Kind hearts are more than coronets,
And simple faith than Norman blood.'
Tennyson.

PREFACE

So beautiful a pastoral county as Warwickshire, the very heart of rural England, affords
charming pictures for the pen of the descrip-
tive writer and the pencil of the artist, and
the wonder is that more writers and painters
have not gone to the sweet and peaceful nooks
of nature to be found there in such abundance. The scenes of rural life comprised in this
volume are written by a native who knows
every mead, stream, hill, cottage, farmhouse,
manor, lane and hedgerow of the ground
traversed, and the writing of them has been
to him a labour of love. The sketch entitled
'Under the Chestnut Tree' describes the unique
and hitherto unrecorded initial meeting of Warwickshire peasants under the historical chestnut

tree at Wellesbourne, when the famous Joseph Arch called the Arcadians to revolt ; but the author has idealised the scene as more in harmony with the beauty of the setting, and has caused the preacher to preach a gospel or content rather than of discontent. If the perusal of these scenes, 'In Russet Mantle Clad,' attracts more attention to the charms of a country life, where true happiness is invariably to be found, his task will have been to him more than ever delightful.

GEORGE MORLEY.

Leamington, 1897.

CONTENTS

Round the Red House Farm—

Under the Chestnut Tree—

Out with the Poachers—

Contents

The Poacher's Friend—

The Two Shepherds—

Rural Merrymakings—

Contents

Round the Red House Farm

A

'THE ONLY TRUE CRITIC OF THE RED HOUSE FARM.'

In Russet Mantle Clad

SCENES OF RURAL LIFE

Round the Red House Farm

> But, look, the morn in russet mantle clad
> Walks o'er the dew of yon high eastern hill.
> *Shakespeare.*

The Red House WHY the farm should be called the 'Red House' I cannot tell, but in all the surveys and maps of the county it is marked out and thus designated. Perhaps it is because it is built of red brick. That seems the only rational explanation of the name. Or it may be so called upon the principle that, as almost all country parishes have a Red House Tavern, so they must almost all have a Red House Farm.

I, who am strictly conservative in nearly all matters relating to the country, have changed

3

the title of that farm. Its name, however, is
merely changed to me, and not to the many
people who occasionally wander round it. To
them it is always the Red House, and always
will be. The laws of the rustics are the laws
of the Medes and Persians; they never change;
they are always the same. As the speech of
the peasant of to-day is the speech of the
peasant of the past, so a name of the past is
the name of to-day.

For myself, who live just on the borders
of Arcadia, I generally call that farm ' the
House with the Five Red Peaks,' because that
farm is so built that at a distance five red
peaks, belonging respectively to the house
itself, and the outbuildings, can be clearly
seen peeping up from among the trees.

It could not be more fitly described than
by the word ' lumbering.' It is lumbering.
It is just one of those roomy, draughty, ungainly and lumbering farmhouses which George
Eliot so well pictured in her Warwickshire
novels. There is no front door to it, and if
that is not an awkward thing, what is? When
you approach it by the only way of approach

there is, you simply walk past the duck pond up to the back door. And upon this there is no knocker.

You see the Red House is an old farm. It was old long before those happy days when I loitered round it, and those visitors who go there are accustomed either to walk straight into the house, or to rap on the outer door with their riding-whips. No knocker is therefore required.

The farm is a typical Warwickshire farm.

People who go closer to the house than the red pond are supposed to be friends. They open the door, enter the farmyard, and walk on into the house. They are known, they are welcome, and the dear old Scotch collie does not bark them off, as he will a suspicious-looking character the moment he sees him.

The
Canine
Critic
AND this is a curious thing. That dog knows as well as if he were a human creature the questionable signs in the appearance of a stranger. He is the only true critic of the Red House Farm.

His master may speak to a tramp, but the collie, having viewed the man from top to toe, and not liking the look of him, will do nothing of the kind. He will growl ominously, or bark outright. He will not even wag his beautiful tail as a sign of peace and amity. He will only keep close behind the heels of his master, with his bright eyes peeping round one of his master's legs, at the person he so profoundly mistrusts.

Upon such occasions I have noticed that he even dares to be disobedient to his master. When the latter says to him rather petulantly, 'Hold yer tongue, canna yer,' that collie will not hold his tongue, but will speak all the more. It is only so, however, when he sees a person of uncouth or forbidding aspect. At other times his canine highness is a most dutiful dog, with a strong love for his master, and a wag of the tail for anyone whose face pleases him.

※ ※ ※

The Good. Easy Farmer SOMETIMES I think the landlord of the Red House Farm was too kind to the dumb creatures of which he was the possessor. Too much kindness, like too much familiarity, breeds contempt. This is as true with regard to animals as human beings, because their instinct is as sharp and their observation as close. Kindness can only rarely be associated with authority. Therefore, if a farmer or other owner of cattle wishes to have dominion over them, kindness must be meted out with a wise though still affectionate hand.

The farmer of the Red House was too lavish in this direction. He was even a slave to his little cob.

☙ ☙ ☙

The
Saucy
Cob
NE day I came round the farm by the footpath on the south side, for that is a pretty, secluded way, and there are many birds to be seen and heard in the hedgerows there, which you do not find in the lanes. Various species of wild flowers, too, are to be gathered there in abundance ; and, as I love to make a posy of these flowers, that is my favourite way.

Upon the morning in question I had reached the last field before the entrance to the long lane coming from the northwards—which is

the only way by which a cart or carriage can
approach the Red House Farm. When near-
ing the end of the ash-strewn walk, and within
earshot of the pigeons cooing on the red peaks,
I heard a stamping of horse's hoofs on the other
side of the hedge—the hedge leading into the
lane.

I also heard a well-known voice saying,
'Now, you canna be thirsty agen, so come out
on it, you young rascal!' Then there was
another stamping, a plunging, and ultimately a
splashing. It was the master of the Red House
wrestling with his saucy cob.

I opened the gate and came out into the
grass lane. There was the gaunt and long
farmer, his legs dangling some distance below
the pony's belly, astride his favourite nag, looking very much like Don Quixote upon the mule.
Both horse and man were pulling in opposite
directions. The horse wanted to go and stand
in the red pond, the man wanted to pass by the
pond altogether.

It was an undignified wrangle, but an amusing
spectacle. When the farmer saw me, he laughed
in such a manner as only robust and healthy

farmers can laugh. 'Whenever we pass this pond,' he said in explanation of the circumstance, 'the young rascal always makes up his mind to go in the pond, an' I suppose he mun go in now.'

Thereupon, with the questionable policy of submitting to things with a bare protest, the farmer let loose the short reins, and the victorious pony walked into the pond. His 'master' on his back seemed more delighted with the cob's stubbornness than displeased with his own folly in giving in so tamely. It was this amusing episode which led me to think that the farmer of the Red House was too kind to his dumb creatures, from the obstinate pony to the stupid white geese being fed up for the market.

The Star- lings as Door- keepers AT the beginning of this paper I said there was no knocker upon the one door, and that a back one, that leads to the House with the Red Peaks. Neither is there; but there is no need for one. You make a mistake if you suppose that there is.

This farm is entirely isolated on every side from all abodes of the human family. It is placed among the foliage of a thickly-wooded country, away from village and town, and a good mile from the nearest church. It is near to a river, close to a large park, and within sight of three or four well-preserved spinneys. During the night and through the small hours of the morning that farmhouse is surrounded by poachers, for the land thereabouts affords them good catches of rabbits and occasional hares. But neither in the night or day is there much human life to be met with at that farm.

You may pass the red pond and go up to the back door many times a day without seeing a man or woman there. You may sit on the dead trunk that lies under the shady lime tree for hours and not be disturbed by any intruder from the house. No human sound reaches you through the buckthorn hedge that grows between the farmhouse and the paddock and huts outside.

But you are watched although you can see no one, and the watchers sometimes serve the purpose of doorkeepers. The fact is, there are several starlings looking down upon you, and if you move too near the tree in which their nest is built, they will soon let you know it.

The starling, however, does not utter so startling an alarm note as the blackbird or the missel-thrush—the ' hoarse-thrush,' as it is called in Warwickshire. If you suddenly surprise either of these birds sitting upon its nest in a ditch, or drinking from a runnel in a spinney, a cry will cleave the air, absolutely startling, coming through the stillness. The intruder is scared by the bird's scream as much as the bird is scared by the approach of the intruder. The starling's notes of alarm do not scare so much as those of the blackbird or missel - thrush, but they are much more irritating.

You see ' the little jackdaw,' as he has sometimes been called, is a very different bird from the throstle or blackbird. He is ten times bolder—when he is in a tree. The starling, like the blackbird, will soon take to his wings if you surprise him on the ground. When he is perched up in a tree his courage is splendid, and he will not easily budge. His eye, too, is keen, and ever on the alert.

If you stand under an elm tree—and there
are many fine ones round the Red House Farm,
for Warwickshire is noted for its majestic elms
—in which a pair of starlings have built their
nest, they will see you although you cannot
see them. When they have young ones they
are more noisy and determined. All the time
you stand under that tree, they will make a
small cawing or rattling kind of noise ; something like the sound from the two bass strings
of a fiddle. But as soon as you have moved
away a few steps from the tree, their creaking
ceases. The starlings have no further cause for
anxiety when you have gone.

The pair of starlings near the back door of
the Red House Farm make a terrible chattering
if you approach too close to their tree. This
cue is taken up by the pigeons on the red tiles,
and seconded by the jackdaws and crows on the
neighbouring trees, or in the air. In a short
time there is such a general bird-chorus that
the hard-hearing labourer, cutting the thistles
in the close, lifts up his heavy head and looks
towards the place where the sound comes from.

He adds to the charm by chiming in with

the words, 'Canna yer stop yer jawing?' But
the birds 'canna' stop until the object of their
alarm has disappeared, so the rustic bends down
again to his thistle cutting. If therefore there
is not a knocker upon the back door of the
Red House Farm, there are sentinels at hand
who can make much more row at the intrusion
of a stranger into private quarters.

**The
Birds'
Fear of
Man**

THE fear of man in the minds
of birds — for a bird has a
mind and all reasoning facul-
ties equally with a human being—is, in some
cases, very vividly portrayed. One of the
most timorous, though apparently daring, birds
is the water-wagtail. This is perhaps because
the wagtail is a rather proud and exclusive
bird. His beauty makes him proud, and his
reserve makes him exclusive. He appears to
prefer the society of his own wife to that of
any other birds in his neighbourhood. Thus,
more than two water-wagtails are not often
seen together, and these are generally united
together in the holy bonds of bird wedlock.

In my perambulations of the Red House Farm I have never seen more than two wagtails together at one time. No doubt there may be occasions when three, four, or even five of these pretty, pied creatures can be seen together; but, as a rule, I believe water-wagtails are not gregarious. In districts nearer the seashore than the shire from which I write, groups of wagtails are common, and Gilbert White speaks of seeing a flock at Selborne; but in more inland haunts they are rarer and are generally only seen in pairs.

The pairs I have seen have invariably been trotting in the vicinity of the duck-pond on the north side of the House with the Red Peaks. In the case of one of these birds— it must have been the male, because that one's plumage was so much finer and more glossy than that of the other—the existence of fear was shown in a marked degree.

It is my custom to take a long walk in the country every morning, before breakfast, in summer and winter. There is something so truly delightful in viewing the wild life of the fields, meadows, lanes and ponds wake up

from its nightly slumbers ; and on the morning in question I was out rather earlier than
usual.

As a rule, the month of April is not remarkable for severe night frosts, but the night
before this morning had been an exception to
the rule. The earth was covered with a silver-
like powder. Every blade of grass was heavy
with it.

In passing through a short lane, the ground
of which was thickly overgrown with grass, on
the south side of the Red House, I saw a
strange little, dark object on the walk before
me. At first it was stationary, and looked like
a piece of dead twig. Then, as I drew nearer,
it ran quite rapidly along the path, having
the appearance of a huge fly with its wings
pulled off. All this time there was an
alarmed twittering from a wagtail in the
nearest tree. This bird, in a very frightened
manner, kept flying down to the object on
the path, and then fluttering back into the
branches.

I then came to the conclusion that the little
running thing, which, as I approached, kept

hopping into the air in its endeavours to fly, was a wagtail — the mate of the one in the tree—with its wings cramped by the frost. Such, indeed, proved to be the case. When I caught the quaint-looking little creature, which panted and struggled in my hands, I found its wings closed as tightly to its sides as if they had been glued there.

But, curiously, it was not so frightened at being unable to fly as it was at being in the hands of a stranger of the human race. After I had dried and attended to its wings as well as the circumstances would allow, I set it down again—much, apparently, to the joy of its mate, who hovered in the air, twittering louder than before, and to its own delight.

The poor invalid wagtail, however, was no better. It gave two or three energetic hops into the air, but it could do nothing more in the way of flying. When I went to pick it up again its fear became intensified. With one of those peculiar body motions observed in the genus Motacilla, the little wagtail made a sudden dart from the bank into the ditch under the hedge, and before I could reach it, it made

a second dart, right into a hole in the sandy
bank in which the hedge grew.

Thinking the foolish creature would be suf-
focated, I got into the ditch and looked into
the hole, the aperture of which was about the
size of a half-crown   There I saw the tip of
the frightened creature's tail, and that was all.
The moment I tried to extricate it, it bored
further into the hole, with the alacrity of the
sand - martin.   Whether the soil was loose
enough for it to bore through the bank and
come out on the other side or not, I cannot
tell.   Some colour was lent to the idea by the
other wagtail flying from the tree into the
field, as if expecting to see its mate come
peeping through the earth on that side—
which I hope and believe it did.

The
Sheep
Meadow
AND here, while writing of the
fear of man entertained by
some birds, I may also note
the same fear existing in sheep.   This, of
course, is varied, according to the circumstances
of the case.   Sheep lying under trees in

B

summer will not rise if you walk quietly by
them. I have done so frequently in the fields
and meadows round the Red House Farm.

So long as you walk leisurely by them,
with no sudden movements which they do
not understand, the sheep will remain in their
recumbent position, chewing the happy cud
of a bright summer's day, with a mind at
peace with all the world, and with no haunt-
ing thoughts of the shambles and the butcher's
knife. But if you move your hand to try
and touch them, they are all up in a moment.
The hearing of sheep is so acute ; more so
than their sense of smell or sight.

When the lambs are a few weeks old, they
lie by the dozen in the long meadow on the
north - east side of the Red House. The
meadow slopes off gradually to the little blue
river, in the sedges of which the reed warbler
makes its home. I think this big, straggling
meadow must at one time have been submerged
with water—when the small brook was of much
greater dimensions than at the present time ;
for there are pronounced undulations in many
places, and in some spots deep gutters, now

"THE SECLUDED RETREAT OF THE DOWAGER OF AYLESFORD."

grown over with grass, as if at some bygone period a large body of water had rested above the meadow.

This idea is quite consistent with the history of the neighbourhood, which, in remote ages was a royal seat—a king of Mercia holding a brilliant Court there. At the date of this sketch it was the secluded retreat of the Dowager Countess of Aylesford. The position of the Red House Farm favours this assumption; for this building and the lands lying south and north of it are boldly placed upon an eminence; whereas the meadows and the fields near the brook are all extremely low-lying, and seem to have been the bed of a moat, which probably surrounded the palace of the ancient Mercian king.

The
Sleep-
less
Ovines
HE meadow is a very luxuriant one, and, as I have said, the lambs when they are a few weeks old are turned into it by the dozen, along with their dams. It is here, on a hot

summer day, that you can test the quickness of the ovine's ear. I have tested them for my own satisfaction, and the curious thing I have found is, that the sheep and lambs know the difference between human and animal sounds when lying apparently fast asleep.

They lie sprawling in the green ridges, breathing heavily. Rooks, starlings and magpies trot about their bodies and peck the insects from their growing fleece. But the ovines do not wake from their afternoon nap. A wag of the ear alone indicates that the lambs know some living thing is about. The curious part of it is that the woolly sleepers appear by instinct to know that the live potterers about them are birds. They know the footfalls.

Now I have tried time after time to put my hand upon one of those sheep or lambs lying in that meadow, and have never succeeded. I have crept up to within a foot of them when they have seemed in that condition known as being 'dead with sleep,' but I think their sleep must be sleepless or as light as the weasel's, for they have never allowed me to touch them. Yet

other creatures, making quite as much noise as
human beings, can perch upon their backs or
hop over them, and they take no notice.

These observations led me to the conclusion
that the greater vibration of the earth from the
tread of a human foot is the reason of the
ovine's suspicion. Another explanation may be
—and, perhaps, this is the correct one—that the
ovine's strong sense of smell warns them of the
approach of him whom they look upon as their
enemy.

The
Three
Lambs:
a Pas-
toral
Tragedy
AS an illustration of downright
fear in sheep, I will describe
a little scene witnessed by me
during one of my rambles round the
Red House Farm.

A flock of ten or twelve white lambs, with
one wicked black one, were all clustered
together at a gate. They were fine Warwick-
shire-bred lambs about four months old, and
were pushing their noses through the bars of
the gate at three other lambs in the next field.
The three solitary lambs bleated plaintively.
They seemed to pine for the companionship

of their sisters and brothers on the other side
of the wooden fence.

Now why, I thought, are those three lambs
shut away from their fellows—their fellows
who seem to pine as much for the three as
the three do for them? What have they
done to have the gate shut upon them? Poor
lambs! in what way can they have transgressed
the laws which the shepherd or the farmer
governs them by, so as to incur their anger
past all hope of relenting.

Have they broken through the limits laid
down for them, such as sheep and lambs often
do, and wandered in the corn or among the
rising turnips? Or are the poor creatures
preparing themselves for the butcher's knife
by getting fat quicker than the rest of the
flock, as some lambs do, and so make a rapid
rush to the end?

This, indeed, seemed to be the cause of
their isolation. Each of the three lambs was
much fatter than the others bleating on the
opposite side of the gate. Their sides hung
down with fat. Their backs were very broad,
and as flat as if the grass-roller from the

Red House had been rolling them down. By the look of their round, big and frightened eyes, it would almost seem as if this was the correct explanation of their enforced estrangement from their companions.

Yes, it is so. Across the verdant meadow, far in the distance by the blue pond where their mother bore them in the spring of the year, can be seen a fleck upon the turf. Two flecks, in fact. The timid eyes of the three fat lambs strained themselves dreadfully to discover what those specks were. Soon the staglike fright depicted in those big eyes showed that the lambs knew, only too well, the form those specks would assume.

One speck was smaller than the other, and seemed closer to the ground. In the prospect it looked like a giant rook walking on the pastures in search of worms. As it comes nearer it assumes more of the appearance of a weasel. Then it looks like a black lamb. At last its identity is revealed — it is the butcher's dog! Yes, and there is the butcher's boy, with his red, hard, unrelenting face, in his blue blouse, and carrying a stick in his hand, with which to beat the three doomed sheep should they not run to the slaughter fast enough to please him.

The dog barks. That bark has betrayed it all, for it is a different bark altogether from that of the collie at the Red House. With one wild, frantic rush, those three overgrown lambs tear round the field. Then with panting sides and despairing bleats they come up to the gate again. They kiss the noses of their companions, as if kissing them a last farewell. They then stay sadly and patiently for the coming of the butcher boy—for they now, by instinct, seem to know the doom that awaits them.

But there—I must stop. The look in the eyes of those pretty, fat lambs will never be effaced from my heart—never be blotted out from my memory.

The Sheep and the Fox-hounds

 I THINK this episode, which I watched with unfeigned regret, is a clear proof of the fear of man entertained by sheep. It also

convinces me that sheep have the power of discrimination.

Consider the condition of their lives. In Warwickshire they have no variation ; no big hills or crags to roam over, which impart a wildness and independence to sheep in more exposed situations. Round the Red House Farm they lead monotonous lives. They browse and sleep with always an ear awake to catch the sound of their enemies—the man and dog. The latter is often the cause of terrible fear to them.

They are especially afraid of a pack of foxhounds. Just as in wilder places the sight of an eagle or kestrel in the sky drives the poor ovines mad with fear, so in the flats of Warwickshire the sheep are filled with dread at the sound of the huntsman's horn or the baying of the foxhounds.

Not so long ago a well-known tenant farmer in this shire had in his possession a flock of forty-three ewes. Seventeen of these proved barren at the lambing season through abortion, caused by being frightened by the hounds when crossing the fields. Foxhunting, therefore, is

regarded by some farmers with grave displeasure ; and when a farmer suffers, through
one season of foxhunting, to the extent of
£20, his displeasure is not to be wondered at.

🔔 🔔 🔔

The
Ovine's
Eye
for
Colour

BUT though so fearful of all dogs,
of whatever size, breed or
colour, I have found, as before
mentioned, that sheep are not fearful
of all human creatures. Their wild eyes and
timid minds are gifted with the qualities of
discrimination.

Though they may never in their lives before
have seen the sight of a butcher's aggressively
blue smock frock, yet the sheep seem instinctively to know what its appearance
portends. The lambs are as frightened at
the sight of it as the old sheep. But no
doubt the matrons of the flock hand down to
the younger ones the tradition of the danger
impending them whenever a blue man appears
upon the pastures.

A woman dressed in blue, red, white, black
or yellow seems not to have the slightest effect

upon a flock of sheep. In such attire a lady
may walk through a whole recumbent herd
without disturbing them; but the moment
they see the boy or man in the blue smock,
they are upon their legs directly, in a state of
great agitation. Tokens like these are sufficient
to show that sheep can not only distinguish
between colours, but between individuals as
well.

The
Swal-
low's
Energy
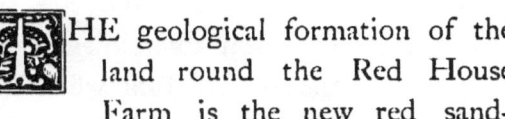HE geological formation of the
land round the Red House
Farm is the new red sand-
stone; and this, perhaps, in some measure
accounts for the warm look of the pathways
in the fields and lanes. That lane, that long
one near the sheep meadow, so luxuriantly
bordered with grass, and filled with moths and
butterflies, which, once a year, and once only,
tastes the edge of the mower's scythe, looks
particularly red after an earnest shower of
summer rain.

The black ash, which is placed on the path in
some places to prevent the foot from slipping,

has the appearance of being decorated. A long, snake-like strip of red forms a gutter upon the black, and when this admixture of earth is softened by the rain to the consistency of pulp, the house swallows begin to carry it away in mouthfuls to the nooks and eaves of the Red House.

I have watched these delicate creatures with growing interest. Their energy is marvellous when the distance they fly is considered. Their patience and perseverance, too, are such as to afford a useful lesson to indolent mortals.

It was at the end of June when I saw them building their nests. The red pond near the farm had no mud round it, because it was full, and the surrounding space consisted of gravel stones upon which no soft earth had collected. The swallows, therefore, were obliged to go more than a quarter of a mile up the lane in search of material for their houses. There the soil was softer, and the ridges made by the carts deeper, so that a plentiful supply of mud could be gathered.

❊ ❊ ❊

The
Swal=
low's
Hardi=
hood

THE swallows that take up their quarters every summer at the Red House are not at all timid. On the north-east side of the farm buildings, towards a clump of nut-bushes, and near to the brook, I found a sand-martin's burrow, from which the two birds flew out in great alarm at my approach. Sand-martins, owing to their love of seclusion, are very shy, and though so much like the house swallow in appearance, are not at all like that bird in their habits.

I thought the swallows, indeed, being so far from the town, would have been frightened at the sight of a human being. But no ; it was pleasant to me to find that they were not. In fact they had the hardihood to quite ignore me altogether, and I was very glad they did, because I wished to watch them in their building operations.

The
Swal=
low's
Industry

I STOOD quite close to the ridges of soft mud, red and black, and the swallows would come and settle within a few feet of me, apparently without the slightest trepidation. When they are building they appear too much in earnest with their work to notice anything or anybody.

With a long sweep or dart from the peaks of the Red House, they skim the pathway of the lane for some distance, then suddenly wheel upward, take a small circle in the air just above the tops of the hedgerows, and come fluttering down boldly upon the heaps of soft mud. They then pull away at the material for their houses. They are so exceedingly quick in their movements, that if you do not observe them closely you will not see that, with two rapid pecks, they have filled their beaks with a wedge of mud, and are darting off to the red nooks again.

Nothing seems to call off the swallow's attention from his architecture. The cry of the landrail, or 'corncrake,' as we call it in Warwickshire, comes up from the fields on each side of the lane, but the swallow takes no heed. If a red cow intrudes upon the soft mud ridges—and the horned cattle *are* often turned loose in that lane, much to the regret and alarm of timorous ladies—the

swallows wheel and dart about them in utter
indifference.   They seem to feel a certain
security in the rapid motions of their wings.
Not easily, indeed, do swallows give way to
fear.

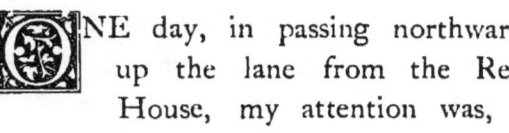

The
Hawk
and the
Swal-
lows

NE day, in passing northward
up the lane from the Red
House, my attention was, I
know   not   how,   attracted   to   an
object in the sky.

The swallows were skimming the ground
and wheeling into the air in all directions,
and with their sharp-sighted eyes must have
seen the quivering thing overhead.   It was
a hawk, but I could not get close enough to
see of what species.   The short wings, however, led me to conjecture that it was a
sparrow-hawk ; and this is the more likely,
because at the time of his appearance in the
sky, a hen from the Red House Farm was
taking her brood of chicks for a walk in the
close, and sparrow-hawks are known to be
extremely fond of chickens.

The hawk in question was poised in the

air at a considerable height, and beyond a
slight movement of the wings, imperceptible
unless watched closely, seemed more like a
sky sign than a bird. He was, in fact, just
preparing to swoop. The swallows and
martins wheeling beneath him must have
been fully aware of his intentions, yet they
betrayed not the slightest fear or the least
concern. When the hawk dropped like a
stone from the sky towards its prey, the
swallows went on darting and wheeling just
the same, though the sparrows scattered in
all directions.

The hawk speedily rose again, having
missed its mark, and made for a neighbouring
spinney in which the cuckoo was merrily
uttering its familiar note.

∿ ∿ ∿

The
Red
House
Cuckoo
WITH regard to the cuckoo, I
have seen many remarks in
print, and heard them made,
which do not in the least coincide with my
experience of this well-known bird. For
instance, I have heard it said and seen it

stated that a cuckoo only utters its cheery notes when flying.

A dear old friend of mine, the widow of a country vicar, whom I should not like to contradict, once emphatically asserted that a cuckoo never spoke when seated in a tree. That lady was the wife of a former vicar of Chilvers Coten, 'The Shepperton' of George Eliot; and, living in such a quaint little village, she had doubtless ample opportunities for studying the peculiar habits of this peculiar member of the feathered race. I can only say that my experience of the cuckoo in the neighbourhood of the Red House Farm, which is several good miles from Chilvers Coten, are not the same as those of the vicar's widow.

I have seen a cuckoo in a tree of Warwickshire elm and heard it utter its note time after time. It has then flown a short distance —for the cuckoo is a restless bird, neither flying nor settling for long together—without uttering a single note. Then, as soon as it had settled again, it began with its cheerful notes as loudly and saucily as ever. I have experienced this many times, and it may be accounted for by the supposition that the habits of the cuckoo may vary according to the condition of the neighbourhood in which it resides.

The Comyn Rookery ROOKS are very plentiful round the Red House Farm. This may be explained by the fact that the whole district is well-timbered, and in some places there are thick clusters of elms, firs and beeches.

These clusters are very attractive to such gregarious and sociable birds as rooks. They are still more attractive when the fields thereabouts are likely to furnish them with provender. And where there are rooks there are jackdaws; and where there are jackdaws there are sure to be starlings. In this neighbourhood there are huge flocks of all these birds; and on the south-west of the Red House there is the remnant of a fir avenue —centuries old—attached to The Comyn, in the top of which these congenerous creatures most do congregate.

If you walk past this rookery about six

o'clock on a summer morning, there is not a
rook to be seen in any of the trees. Only
their nests can be descried in the knotty
clumps of the dark firs. The rooks, in
fact, are out on their feeding grounds, and
if you go farther into the landscape you will
see scores of them in the lower meadows or
on ploughed lands.

After breakfast—that is, about nine or ten
o'clock—you will find all the rooks returned
to the rookery again, and making so great a
chattering that you can hardly hear the sound
of your own voice. Having frequently passed
the rookery when the birds have been con-
tending in heated debates, I have wondered
how the lady of The Comyn, who lives there
—a widow with her young children—could
stand the noise. It begins during prayers,
and continues all through the music lesson.

The
Fallen
Rook-
ling
A YOUNG rook fallen out of its
nest, if it is not much hurt, will
stand stock still and let you
approach quite near to it.

On one of my circles of the Red House, I was surprised, upon looking ahead, to see a black-bird upon the pathway. Those who know the habits of rooks are aware that upon the first sight of a human creature Mr Rook will not budge. He does not in the least care for Mr Human Creature. He will go on digging with his long, spear-like beak for the food which he cannot always find. To see a man or woman, or even a boy, merely walking in the ordinary way has no fear for him at all. But if you lift your walking-stick ever so slowly in the air, Mr Rook is off. Away he flies with his wife and children—his sisters, his cousins and his aunts.

I raised my stick towards the young rookling on the pathway, but he never stirred ; only stood looking at me with his big, black eyes in a very confused manner. There was a terrible cawing and flapping in the trees overhead, which told me plainly that the rook on the ground was a young one, and his parents were alarmed at the danger he was in, having fallen from the parental nest.

Before he has properly learnt the use of his
wings, the young rook is a foolish and clumsy
creature.   This young one nearly broke his
neck through his own clumsiness.   Just as I
was about to pick him up and see what was
the matter, the stupid biped jumped in the air,
wallowed along for a few yards, and toppled
headlong over into a patch of long grass.
When I found him, he lay as still as if he had
taken his last fly round the Red House Farm.

Only his eyes were alive, and they looked at
me so piteously that I knew he must have
hurt himself.   I picked him up carefully and
carried him farther down the meadow, where
he would run no danger of being stoned to
death by inhuman schoolboys.   There I laid
him in the grass, and soon had the satisfaction of seeing the parent birds come fluttering
lower down the fir and beech trees in search
of their venturesome offspring.

In Warwickshire there is a little folk-lore
concerning rooks.   It is considered a sign of
impending illness or death for a rook to settle
on a town house.   To see one solitary rook
flying is regarded as a prognostication of ill-

luck. In the rural parts, and among town
children, there is an implicit belief in the
old tradition that rooks go to school. My
own observations round the Red House Farm
have almost made me a convert to that belief.

❦ ❦ ❦

The
Rooks
at
School

ABOUT the elevations, for you
cannot call them hills, that lie
on the north-east of the farm,
are several basins or 'coombs' of good size.
These are generally on pasture land, because
they would be somewhat difficult to cultivate.
I have stood at a convenient place, hidden
from the birds' view, and watched them fly
by the score into these grassy basins. Their
time for conducting this performance is generally in the hottest part of a summer's afternoon, when, owing to the heat, the sheep,
cows and grazing horses are lying out in
the shade, sleeping.

More than once I have crept silently and
close to the basins into which I saw the rooks
fly, and there a sight has appeared which fully
realises the idea that rooks go to school.

All the birds were sitting in a circle round
the basin, and in the middle of the ring were
two or three rooks strutting about, with more
than a rook's usual importance.   Just like
children at school, all the rooks were chattering to one another, in short, sharp, jerky
notes.   Nothing more like a school have I
ever seen than those sunny afternoon con-
fabulations of Warwickshire rooks.

Whenever they are disturbed, they rise in a
body and wheel off to another basin to re-
sume their interrupted lesson in the art of
conversation.   It may be that the one, two
or three rooks in the middle of the ring were
entertaining the company with an account of
their adventures.   At any rate, these summer
afternoon bird performances give colour to,
and strengthen belief in, the rural tradition
that rooks, among other curious things, go
to school.

✳ ✳ ✳

The Hedge-rows and Ditches

THE hedgerows round the Red
House Farm, in spring, summer and autumn, are things
of beauty to the lover of Nature.   They

are generally composed of English hawthorn,
which in June bears a white flower, and are
cut low after the new fashion of hedge trim-
ming—a fashion which I do not in the least
admire.   In many places, however, the crab-
tree, the elder and the wild rose have a
charm which the green hawthorn does not
possess.

The ditches are garlanded with flowers—
the cowslip, the primrose, the lady smock,
the wild hyacinth (called in Warwickshire 'the
bluebell') and the periwinkle.   In the bottom
of the ditches, cuckoo points, familiarly known
as 'lords and ladies,' are found in abundance.
'Tis here that the gatherer of wild flowers will
find a good harvest.   'Tis here that we may
go hand in hand with Christopher Marlowe,
and say,—

> 'And I will make thee beds of roses,
> And a thousand fragrant posies.'

Under the Chestnut Tree

Under the Chestnut Tree

A Gathering of Arcadians

Give me again my hollow tree,
A crust of bread, and liberty.
Pope.

The Chestnut Tree HOW the time goes! But the old chestnut tree pays no heed to the time, and the time pays no heed to it. Unlike the poor race of men who congregate under it, who change and pass away, that tree is immutable. It changes only with the seasons.

In February when the golden plover and the curlew fly by night from the seashore to inland haunts, that tree is naked. A little later it buds, then bursts into bright green leaves; then is glorified all over with white blossoms; then sheds its fruit; lastly its leaves, and becomes once more the naked tree it was in those early February days, many centuries ago—a work superior to man in many respects.

43

It is not exercising the imagination too much
to suppose that under this very chestnut tree,
where on this particular morning in February
of the year 1872 the labourer in his smock
frock is gathering in quite unusual crowds, our
own Shakespeare halted to take a rest, when on
that long tramp of his to Babylon, more than
three hundred years ago. He would have to
pass this tree on his road from Stratford-on-
Avon to Rugby, as it lies in a direct line between
those towns; and when he passed that way he
was doubtless attracted to its welcome shade;
for when in leaf this chestnut tree is a beautiful
retreat for the traveller.

Whether this was really so or not cannot be
determined, but it is pleasant even to think that
it was; for those of us who are Warwickshire
born derive fascinating pleasure from walking,
or fancying we are walking, in the footsteps of
him who was born near, though not within
hailing distance of this chestnut tree.

A Chill February Morning IN the cold month of February, when the little ponds of the village are covered with silver ice, and unadorned with the merry flotilla of ducks; when the winds are sometimes very cutting, so much so that even the sturdy peasant woman has to cover up her fat, red arms and tie her cotton bonnet closer round her throat; when the cowman is never so warm as when he is carrying a truss of hay from the rickyard into the stable, or at such times as he is in the barn milking the cows—for alas ! for the romance of village life, the milkmaid is now almost only a pretty vision of the past; when the clouds look burdened with snow, and the rooms of the great, lumbering, though picturesque, farmhouses are glowing with rosy light and warmth from immense wood fires; when inside the house is better than the outside, and when even the wayward fowls, creatures often as hard as winter, and as indifferent to all weathers as the unhoused beggar, think it best to tuck themselves up close together in their own hen-roost ; on the morning of such a month as this, something unusual

must be in the wind to bring out so many sons
of the soil—men who earned their bread by the
sweat of their brows, and lived in pretty little
thatched huts on the waste or by the side of a
wood; there must also be some peculiar attraction to be found under the aforesaid chestnut
tree, for the labourers, their buxom wives and
squat children, are all going in that direction.

A Group
of Rus-
tics
THERE is a small group here
just crossing over from the
Ham Meadow which will re-
pay the onlooker for giving it a little attention.

It consists of five people—three men, one
woman and a shock-headed girl of about ten
years, who, despite the keenness of the wind, has
no hat upon her head; the back of her frock,
too, owing to the absence of hooks and eyes, is
flying open, thus serving as a door by which to
let in the air upon the child's sharp blade
bones.

The woman of the group, one of those well-
fed, red-cheeked, comely-looking women, who

would win a prize in an exhibition of healthful
specimens of humanity; a woman who, though
' no scholard,' has always a well-oiled tongue by
her, ready for use, is evidently the mother of the
child.

✼ ✼ ✼

Rustic
Collo-
quial-
isms HE looks down at the small
ragamuffin out of a cotton
bonnet that extends several
inches over her face, and says, in that loud voice
peculiar to peasants,—

' Mercy on us! Look at our 'Anner. No
hat on her yed, an' her frock all open at the
back — an' a morning like this, too. As if
you hanna big enough to fast' your own frock
up.'

' There inna no hooks nor eyes on, mither,'
said little Hannah, looking up at her mother
boldly, 'so I couldna do it.'

' Couldna you ope your chops then, an' let
me know as you'd lugged the 'ooks an' eyes
off?' said the mother, with an angry look at
' 'Anner,' as she dragged the child to her, took
a large pin out of her shawl, and pinned up the
back ventilation in the child's frock.

'Now, you'd better goo an' fetch summat to put on yer yed, or 'appen you'll catch a fine coldt.'

'Mither, I donna want ought on my yed. I hanna coldt a bit,' answered the young hoyden, with a vigorous shirk of her loose shoulders, as she ran bounding on in front of the group, her hair flying disorderly in the wind. She was one of those hardy daughters of the country that are always used to roam in the open in all weathers; and no doubt what she said was perfectly true, for village children, when in good health, rarely stand or saunter long enough to allow the blood to congeal in their veins.

'Your 'Anner aint no nesh 'un, Mrs Abel,' said the youngest of the three men who accompanied the woman and her child. 'She'll mak' a sturdy 'ooman, she 'ull.'

'Jest the right sort, Josh, for to emmegrate to Caneder wi',' joined in another of the group —a man who, by his looks and the foul condition of his boots, followed the occupation of farm waggoner.

The man addressed as 'Josh' was evidently

the father of the child, and the husband of
Mrs Abel.   He was very sturdily built, with
a face and neck almost the colour of Farmer
Norman's roan bull.   At the allusion to his
daughter and Canada, he turned his slow gaze
upon the speaker, and then upon the fat face
of his wife, and grunted out rather than
spoke,—

'Well, Yethard, boy, if the gaffer donna put
my wages up a bob or two, I reckon as me
an' the misses an' the gel 'ull 'ave to goo to
Canedar, or some place as is different to this.
We're harty folks, we are, all three on us, an'
we canna do so well on eighteenpence a day.
'Owever you can do it, Aaron,' he said to the
youngest of his companions, 'wi' your five nippers, is more nor I can mek out.'

''Tis a close shave for us, Josh, I can tell
thee,' responded the young man.   'But you
see the master sends us down some bits from
the house, an' meks up me wages i' that way.
If he dinna, by Gosh! I donna know how we
should goo on.   Should soon 'ave to goo to
Poor House, I reckon,' he added with a broad
grimace.

D

The Halting Rustic THOSE who have any acquaintance with rustics have no doubt noticed how halting and intermittent their talk is, even when it is encouraged and aided by the contents of the third quart pot. The peasant is a being whose mind moves as slowly as his own agricultural waggon, and it is some time before he can grasp the meaning of a sentence.

Whether it is that the countryman's organ of sense is permanently dull from need of exercise, or that he is preparing himself with wisdom before he speaks, it is certain that he is a long time between his periods of conversation. He will halt suddenly, take his pipe from his mouth, stare blankly at the speaker, look down upon the ground, hobble a few steps along, and then once more come into contact with words.

It was in this way that Joshua Abel behaved immediately upon the conclusion of his friend Aaron's remarks.

This same young rustic, the odd man about the farm, rejoicing in the scriptural name of

'Aaron,' was notorious in the village as the
person who had the least wages and the most
children. His wife was a winsome country lass,
gamesomely inclined, and as fat as the flitches
of bacon that hung in the kitchen of Farmer
Joyce ; but, as the profane farmer, the man of
crops and cattle, often said, 'her were too fast
a breeder to do any mon any good.' Certainly
Mrs Martin, for such was the name of Aaron's
'missis,' was frequently in need of Dame Win-
cote, the village nurse.

Aaron had five children 'in no time,' as all
the neighbours said, and the actual wages he
received in money were but nine shillings a
week. To some of the villagers, therefore, and
notably to Joshua Abel—who, besides being an
agricultural labourer, was by turns an earth-
stopper, a mole catcher, and, when occasion
offered, a poacher — it was a mystery 'how
Aaron Martin, with them five blessed nippers,
could mek a do on it at all.'

This morning, in going to the chestnut tree
to hear 'the preaching,' Aaron, as we know,
had slipped out a word or two about having
'bits from the master' at the great house, and

it was those few words that had the effect of stopping the speech of Joshua Abel, and at the same time of starting it again, for the word 'bits' angered him more than if anyone had called him a fool.

Those were the days when the farmer paid his men partly in money and partly in kind, and by that method imagined that he was doing the peasant good and himself no harm ; but during the winter months some stir had been made in the villages thereabout with reference to this perquisite system, which some persons had the hardihood to say 'oughter be put down.'

❖ ❖ ❖

More Rural Collo- quial- isms
JOSHUA ABEL had imbibed deeply of the new doctrine, and it was this that checked and then started again his speech when in conversation with Aaron Martin.

'Bits,' he sniffed out, with an air of the greatest contempt, lifting his sleepy eyes to the face of Aaron. 'It's this "bits" system, my butties, as is a-making our case such a hard 'un. Why donna the farmers give us ourn

right wage, an' lave us to buy what us likes
ournselves i' the way o' vittles?' And he
ground his ashplant in the earth by way of
emphasising the dislike he had for that form
of labour payment.

'Eh! Joshua,' chimed in Mrs Abel, from
the depths of her cotton bonnet, 'if we was to
'ave to buy our own vittle allaways, we shouldna
be able to 'ave a bit o' partridge, or pheesant, or
hare, or rabbit, as we does now an' agen from
the gaffer's house. I couldna buy such things,
laddie, boy, if your wage was as much agen as
it am. Besides, I shouldna be able to walk to
Arwick or Brookington for every little thing as
us wanted. I'm fond on a bit o' pheesant, or
partridge, or hare, or rabbit, I am, an' I know
it does me good.'

'Now, Bess,' said her husband, with a rather
angry glance down the tunnel of her bonnet
into her face, 'I never axed you for your
'pinion on the matter o' perquisites, 'cause
wommen know nothing about 'em. As for a
bit o' partridge and such like, canna ye,' he
added, lowering his voice somewhat, and speaking as if confidentially to his wife, 'canna ye

'ave a bit o' that wi'out 'aving it from the
gaffer's table? I hanna so fond on 'aving other
folkses leavings, I hanna. Let 'em eat they're
own orts. But look, butties, yon's the old
chestnut, an' hang me if Joey inna up in't,
praching a'ready. Come, let's push on ! Yander's
our 'Anner, right bang up agen Tim Jordan's
cart. Trust that gel for gettin' her nose in
front of things.'

❦ ❦ ❦

The Gathering of Arcadians
THE rural quartette thus put
on a spurt, if indeed the slow
increase observable in their
strides could be called a 'spurt,' for
the gait of the rustic is as slow and halting as
his gaze and speech, and in a short time the
group was out of the meadow, and the gate
shut behind it. The four rustics were eager to
hear 'the praching.'

Immediately in front of them, with its long,
finger-like branches, naked as yet of leaves,
shooting well up into the leaden sky, stood the
old chestnut tree. It had rooted itself, some
centuries ago, on the north side of the high-
road, and now towered itself aloft and looked

down on the southern meadows—intersected
here and there with little silver streams—with
the pride and vigour of a patriarch who has
won a memorable victory over Time.

In the summer, when that tree is clothed
with leaves, it is a beautiful shade from the
sun, and a useful shelter from the rain during
transient showers ; but in the winter, in the
bleak February days when that tree is leafless,
it is like an old man whose fleshless limbs are
left bare and shivering to the cruel storm.

On this chill morning, when the wind must
have pierced to the very marrow of the people
who were out in it, that chestnut tree would
not have been appreciated as a guard from the
wind, even by the village lurcher. Yet the
men, women and children, who congregated
there in such large numbers, seemed impervious
to it, although at times it lifted their hats, caps
and bonnets, and shook the 'perricuts' of the
women as a dog would shake a rat.

Drawn up to the trunk of the tree was an old
carrier's cart that looked much the worse for
wear. The cover, which had obviously not
tasted tar or paint for years, had a little window

at the back, through which old Tim Jordan,
whose cart it was, could peer when he heard
anybody 'coming on his track,' as he called it.

The splash-board was gone, and also one of
the steps by which persons ascended, the mode
of reaching the interior of the cart being by
placing the foot upon the wheel. Both shafts
were still attached to the cart, but the end of
one was splintered, and the other had been broken
off near to the body of the cart, and roughly
mended by Caleb Ash, the village blacksmith.

Horseless the old carrier's cart stands on this
chill February morning, propped up with a
chump of wood under each shaft. There are
as many holes in the bottom of it as there were
slime pits in the Vale of Siddem. If any crafty
boy had gone beneath it, as a sort of shelter from
the wind, he would have seen many feet of varied
sizes, covered with boots of all sorts and con-
ditions, moving about over the holes.

They were the feet of the supporters of Mr
Joseph Bridge, a man whose rather big person-
ality occupied the whole of the front of the cart,
while his followers were wedged in at the back,
not seen, only through the holes in the bottom

of the cart, and heard only by the shuffling of
their boots, and their constant ' 'Eere ! 'Eeres ! '
when the preacher said aught that met with
their approbation.

A village gathering is very different to a
crowd in town, and no doubt the gathering
under the chestnut tree was, in many respects,
an unusual one. At this there was no hostile
force, no organised opposition. Life in villages
then, although but rather more than two decades
ago, was more purely Arcadian than at the
present time, and the art called ' heckling ' was
not even in its initial stages.

Though this gathering, from the point of
view of some of the restless spirits there, was
practically held for the purpose of setting class
against class—in other words, for making the
farmer understand that the labourer was something more than an ass, to be beaten and left
short of food—it was abundantly of one mind
in point of enthusiasm to hear 'the preaching.'
It was also almost entirely made up of one
class—the class so well represented by Joshua
Abel and Aaron Martin; not forgetting plump
Bessie Abel and the gallivanting ' 'Anner.'

As the eye surveyed the group so comfortably wedged round Timothy Jordan's superannuated cart, it could rest upon nothing but smock frocks, cord trousers tied at the knees, and red faces, some of which had doubtless procured their colour from the taproom of the ' Red House.' There was not a single figure there suggestive of the man of cattle and acres. The only connecting link between this gathering of Arcadians and the farming interest appeared in the form of a red-mottled cow; who, doubtless perplexed at the unusual sight, was hanging her neck over the hedge of the Ham Meadow, staring curiously with her big, round eyes.

To her vision, as to the vision of the congregated peasants, the flourishing figure of Joseph Bridge, protruding from the awning of the carrier's cart, was at that moment the most important figure in the big world, of which the little village of Dellbourne was the eye and the centre.

When the small group which we have just left behind had come close up to the improvised rostrum, Mr Joseph Bridge was 'speechifying to some tune,' as Joshua Abel grunted into his wife's ear, as she squeezed her portly figure among the mass of agricultural concrete there and then congregated.

~ ~ ~

A Bucolic Felix Holt JOSEPH BRIDGE was evidently a man of some account in the neighbourhood, for the labourers when they were at the bottom of the third quart pot in the bar parlour of the 'Red House,' were accustomed to speak of him as 'Joey'; and to address a person by an abbreviation of the Christian name is surely a mark of especial familiarity. Although in his more youthful days—he was now a man entering the middle stage of existence—this preacher had turned his hand to the ploughshare, and had doubtless often fetched Farmer Joyce's cows up from the long meadow, he was, as his listeners were always ready to affirm, 'a cut above them in the eddication line.'

Circumstances had, perhaps, much to do with shaping the ends which he had reached. While yet a boy, that Methodism of which George

Eliot has so good an account in *Adam Bede*,
was rampant in the district in which he lived;
and he, among others, caught the fever.   From
being the passive listener he speedily became
the active preacher, and with his feet upon
many village greens within a little circle of
Dellbourne had he exhorted his hearers to
accept the simple tenets of his faith.

And there he stands looking out of Tim
Jordan's cart, waving his arms sometimes to
the crowd, in the mood of a man who wishes
to give force to an uttered sentiment; at
others, bringing his fairly big fist down upon
the blockboard of the cart with violent earnestness—as if he were knocking a spike of
common sense into the granite craniums of his
bucolic listeners.

The
Preach-
ing
'ES,' he said, as he carefully
wiped back the dark curls
from his forehead with a red
and white cotton handkerchief, upon the corner
of which was worked the letters ' J. B.,' in
white silk, by the deft fingers of his good,

homely wife, 'it *is* better, as the Preacher
saith in the words of my text, to have a dry
morsel and quietness therewith, than an house
full of sacrifices with strife. Ah! my dear
brothers and sisters—for you are morally as
much my brothers and sisters as though we
all belonged to one family—when will you
learn that comforting and cheering truth?
When will you be able to enjoy the blessed
fruits of contentment, free from strivings, free
from complainings—with a light heart and a
merry countenance? When will you cease to
sigh for this world's goods? When will you
cease to lament for what you call your poverty?
Why, my dear friends, out of the meanest
hovel in Dellbourne is obtained as fair a sight
of Heaven as from the most gorgeous palace!
Is not that a lovely thought? Does it not
comfort you to think of it?'

'It do, Joseph, it do,' murmured a dozen
or more voices in the crowd, among which
might be heard the deep bass of Joshua Abel,
deeply impressed with the truth and eloquence
of the preacher.

'It does indeed, my dear fellow villagers

—*all* of us, myself among the number, for I am one of you. I was born in that thatched cottage yonder; I have worked with you; I have scared rooks from the fields for fourpence a day when a boy; I have driven the plough for two shillings a day when a man; and I have looked through the doll's-house windows of my little home and seen above me the beautiful heavens smiling upon the labour of my hands, just as gloriously as if I'd been a prince in a palace; and then I've been so glad and contented to live that I could have leapt over the wheat ricks in front of the housen with very joy at the Lord's goodness to me. Poverty indeed! Why, my dear lads, you're richer than an earl in his castle, if you've only got content in your hearts.'

'Right, Joseph, right!' came the deep-mouthed commentary from many voices in the group of now earnestly attentive listeners.

'Yes, dear brothers and sisters, if you've got contentment in your hearts, you've got that which money can't buy, for the greater the wealth the greater the cares and discontent. Better by far is it, as the Preacher says, to

have an handful with quietness than both the
hands full with travail and vexation of spirit.
Listen to this, too, the words of a Warwickshire boy who has stood under this very tree
where we are now standing, the words he put
into the mouth of a queen,—

> ' " Verily
> I swear, 'tis better to be lowly born,
> And range with humble livers in content,
> Than to be perked up in a glist'ring grief
> And wear a golden sorrow." '

'Ah! 'tis so, 'tis so ; 'tis the trewth he's
tellin' on us,' murmured soft voices of women
and the deep voices of men, touched with the
rugged force of the preacher.

'I'm glad to hear you saying so, my dear
brothers and sisters,' continued Joseph, with
redoubled earnestness and a moistness gleaming
in his eyes. 'I love you for it. I am afraid
you and I, and all of us, are not grateful
enough for the blessed mercy of the Saviour.
Oh! what grace, what love, what riches He has
given us. Look at your lot—is it not enviable?
In the midst of beautiful green fields, waving
trees and crystal watercourses, you pursue your

daily labour, singing, as you ought to, in the delight of your hearts all the day long. What a happy life yours should be ! You have health, strength, beauty, and a freedom from the eating cares which others only too surely know. Be satisfied, dear friends, with your lowly lot. Lift up your hearts in gratitude to the loving Jesus. There is no virtue, no happiness in a life devoid of contentment. Angels are happy only because they are good. Be good, my brothers, and then you will be happy ; and remember this, there is not an individual human scarecrow among you but has a life given him out of Heaven, with eternities depending on it ; for *once* and no second time. Now join with me in one lovely verse,—

> ' " Judge not the Lord by feeble sense,
> But trust Him for His grace ;
> Behind a frowning Providence
> He hides a smiling face." '

With many a tear-stained cheek, and voices quivering with emotion, those gathered Arcadians sang those lines with a greater faith than they had ever had in the grace of God and the virtue of contentment.

Out with the Poachers

I

'THE LAZY LITTLE RIVER WHICH GURGLES OVER A PEBBLY BED.'

Out with the Poachers

Now fades the glimm'ring landscape on the sight,
And all the earth a solemn stillness holds,
Save where the beetle wheels his drony flight
And drowsy tinklings lull the distant folds.

Gray.

The Coombe LOOKED at from the northward, the Red House Farm, in central Warwickshire, lies in a veritable coombe.

There are elevations — not entitled to the dignity of being termed 'hills,' in the sense of a hill's magnitude—all round it. The golf hills in the north are the nearest to the farm, and form a northern belt to the building and its outhouses. A golfer peering through the window of the rustic Club house, built upon the ridge, looks down upon the roof and red peaks of the Red House Farm—jutting out here and there from among the ash, oaks and elms that thickly environ it—as though he were almost looking into a deep valley.

67

The Rook's Ground HE rook flies slowly over that stretch of landscape, so well wooded and well watered. It is his feeding ground. There he comes in large flocks, and covers the chocolate-coloured earth —newly thrown up by the plough—with rank upon rank of black forms, wagging over the undulations like numberless small buoys on a sea of clay.

He regards himself as safe from intruders there, from the herds of little town urchins who shout at him and frighten him so, just when he is engaged in the delicate operation of breaking a fine, fat, red worm. Safe from everything (for there are spinnies close at hand) except the stray shot of a poacher, who grubs in a ditch, and lets fly at him without a license. This is not fair to the rook.

The Man in the Ditch HAT man in the ditch, however, with clay-smirched smock, battered hat, short cutty pipe, and with halting gait—caused some

years since by the shots from a gamekeeper's
gun ; not on the Red House Farm, for there
are no keepers there—thinks that the rook is
not fair to him.

He is not foolish enough—not by any means
such a fool as he looks. His rookship is crafty,
and he has a keen eye, even when as high
again in the sky as the elm tree under which
the poacher is crouching, and from which the
nozzle of his firearm pokes out in threatening
attitude, ready to belch forth smoke, fire and
shot.

No, the rook has far too much intelligence
for the patience of this winged member of the
poaching tribe. It is, in fact, remarkable how
the rooks in those parts seem to know the
hiding-places of their enemies. If it is not
their knowledge of the poacher's whereabouts, it
is their hawklike eyesight which often enables
them to clear out of harm's way.

'See that, sir, see that?' said the poacher to
me as I stood watching him by the side of a
stunted elm tree, which had been split clean
open by the lightning. 'Did take note on
that? Lor, sir, talk about sense ; I should

think as the rooks hereabouts 'ave got more on
that than some on these kids and teachers at
the Board Schools.   Here's another, sir, flying
lowish—look, just over the hedge yon.   You
twig him now?'

A big, heavy-bodied rook, with a beak as
yellow as a corn-stalk, and wattles as white
as the flower of broccoli, was steering his way
through the air, with flapping wings and
stretched-out neck, right over the spot in
which his enemy was crouching, ready to make
'dead game' of him (preparatory to rook pie)
as soon as he came within range of his firearm.

The grubbing poacher, dithering with suppressed excitement as he watched the rumbling
approach of the ungainly bird, and trying as
much as possible to screen himself from the
rook's view, was so unfortunate as to show
the peak of his snuff-coloured, clay-stained,
soft felt hat, together with the nose of his
gun, which, in the emotion of the moment,
he inadvertently permitted to emerge from
beneath the drooping boughs of the elm tree
about the length of two inches.

'See him?' the poacher ejaculated, letting

his weapon fall out of position for firing, and
making his face as ribbed and wrinkled as the
ploughed field opposite, 'See him now? He's
a knowing critter, wonderful knowing. He
wunt let you get a shy at him no-how. Not
if you were to sit in top on the tree. Not
if he sees half an inch on the muzzle poking
out from the leaves. He's an unaccountable
cute 'un.'

And so he was. The bird came towards
the tree, flapping his heavy wings with as much
leisure as the arms of a windmill take their
revolving course, when suddenly he swerved
aside and shot out eastward, with astonishing
briskness—clean out of reach of the unlicensed
poacher's gun.

In less than ten minutes old Mr Rook was
towering high in his native element, joyous at
having espied the nozzle of that fowling-piece
and the peak of that battered hat, flying gaily
to his native rookery ; where, when he had
reached it, he would unfold to his sisters,
his cousins and his aunts, and also to the
members of his own family, the tale of how
the quickness of his eye had saved him from

death and a pie. There would be much
chattering in the rookery that afternoon.

❦ ❦ ❦

The
Black
Lane HIS lane where the poacher
lurked, called 'the Black
Lane' by the little children
of Brookington's suburban courts and alleys,
was the favourite meeting-place of the nocturnal tribe.

It was not a black lane. It was green and
wide, and shady each side with the tall elms
for which Warwickshire is noted. There was
nothing black about it but the pathway, and
that was periodically strewn with ashes—
alternately by the farmer and the county
authority. On this slender ground it was
christened 'the Black Lane' by the roving
youngsters, and I have no doubt it will remain
'the Black Lane' until the end of the chapter.

There was a grass waste on the south side,
about two yards in width. Here the Bohemian,
or his son, brought the donkey. Often, in
passing through that lane towards the lowland
in which the Red House is placed, you can see

the docile creature browsing at his ease ; while,
at a distance, is the Bohemian's son, lazily
stretched out along the turf, playing at pitch
and toss with himself and two pennies.

Every evening, as regularly as the evening
comes, the tribe of men who make a profession of poaching can be seen shambling
along that lane. It is a motley crew, varied
in age as in colour and physiognomy. The
unlicensed rook-shooter is one of them, and
it is perhaps on his account that they shamble.
The place where the 'danged keeper' winged
him is sometimes painful, according as the
weather is, and he cannot keep up with the
rest. So they slouch for him, and shamble
for him, and move as if next week would do
for anything.

At the east end of 'the Black Lane,' the
slouching brotherhood made a halt. The spot,
at that hour and in that uncertain light, looked
like the entrance to a wood. The lane was
well timbered, and at this end, where the
poachers stood looking out over their hunting
ground, two trees met in overhanging embrace,
casting a dense shadow along the lane.

A long, narrow wood with a sweeping curve westward—that is how the lane looked ; and the knot of men, halting in the shadowy alcove, would, to the stranger's eye, have the appearance of woodmen going home from their work—axeless and timberless.

***

The Poacher's Dog

BUT a dog was with them. Not the black and white, half sheep-dog creature, the companion of the woodman, curling himself up on the woodman's coat, and sleeping there all day ; with only an occasional bark to the infrequent stranger, to show that he is alive. No, not that kind of dog.

He is a respectable, honest, well-behaved, frank sort of fellow, not at all ashamed to look anyone in the face, even if it were a king. No, the poacher's companion is quite a different creature, although it is of the canine breed, and walks on four legs.

So far as the dusky light will permit you to see, there is the lurcher, by that stump which, when this lane was a bridle path, was the gate-post. It is as dark as the stump itself, and quite as motionless. It never barks, and scarcely ever moves. You almost wonder whether it can be alive; whether it is not a bronze dog, like some of those on the door-steps of Brookington mansions.

It is only when the poachers move that you can recognise it as a living thing. Then it slides along between their legs, silently, stealthily, the most melancholy creature that crawls under the light of the moon.

To me, who have often seen that lurcher, there always seems something unearthly about it; some nameless something which makes you creep when you look at it. The dog itself appears to be ashamed to have its face scanned by any human creature other than a poacher.

A curse seems upon it. It writhes under a ban which cannot be lifted. It is a doomed dog. Full of elfish craft; more human than canine; more devilish than all. Poor creature, it drops its head and slides off, goblin-like, when you look at it. Once only it lifts its face, and that is enough.

UT that dog's scent is wonderful. In this respect it has the instinct of the bloodhound. Only it does not scent blood. It is the poachers it scents, and they may be street lengths from it, but it is sure to find them. Its track is as deadly certain as the redskin's.

One dark October night, darker than usual for that time of the year, the crew of poachers shambled on their nightly prowl about ten o'clock. There were no stars in the welkin, not a single light with which to enable them to kill their rabbits or to pluck a partridge on the spinney stile.

Orders had been left with the wife of the poacher, gentle lily of a woman to be mated with so rough a master, who owned the animal, not to loose it from the house until they had been gone twenty minutes, the time it took them to shamble to the east end of 'the Black Lane.' The poacher was desirous of testing his lurcher in the science of nocturnal geography, which he had paid great pains to teach him, and also regarding his scent.

The wife of the poacher obeyed her orders
to the letter and the minute.   Poor thing,
she had painful memories of what disobedience
meant.   There were marks on her cheeks and
brow, which even time would never erase—
the caresses of her loving husband.   She therefore released the lurcher in twenty minutes,
and with the words, 'Find him,' sent the
animal on his weirdsome errand.

Like a thing of evil, with nose to the
ground, and thin body writhing as if disturbed by some hidden emotion, the dog made
his way down the passage leading from the
poacher's dwelling.   Down one street, along
another, and up a third it went, just in the
same position, never raising an eye to the
traveller who might be passing at the time.

Sniffing along the ground, with something
of the serpent about it, it pursued its silent
course over the red hills, up the green ones,
and onward to the clap gate leading to 'the
Black Lane.'

There the poachers, waiting under the green
alcove, for they could not proceed without
the dog, strained their eyes, and saw the

creeping, crawling thing wriggling itself towards them at a rapid rate through the dusk, until it grovelled in the black dust at its own master's feet, and licked his hand.

❦❊❦

The Poacher's Natural- ism THIS invaluable member of the poacher's brood having arrived upon the scene, and received a pat on its narrow belly from the big, hard fist of every man there, the tribe moved off, slowly and silently, to their hunting ground in the Red House coombe.

It is not given to poachers to admire Nature's aspects at night-time. In the daylight, when time hangs heavy on their hands, they may show, or appear to show, a half-hearted interest in the beauties of the landscape around them.

Sitting on a stile, or lounging against one, in the manner affected by these sons of Ishmael, they will profess to admire the graceful shape of the hills, the varied colouring of the foliage, and the square stone tower of a village church

peeping from the verdure of a lovely coombe.
Whether this is pretence or not, it is difficult
to say, for the poacher has a way of making
you think he is in earnest.

At night-time the case is different. He is
then on business, and not pleasure bent. Then
he has no time or patience to look upon the
landscape in its cloudy mantle. The rabbits
are out in their hundreds in the coombe close,
and he is anxious to peg the nets and begin
killing.

☙ ☙ ☙

Peasant and Poacher IN single file, with the indispens-
able dog walking solemnly
behind, they stalk across the
field of vetches like a column of shadows from
spirit land. The waggoner of the Red House
Farm has long been sleeping the sleep of contentment in that little cot on the golf hill, in
the little windows of which the white curtains
appear like faces in the gloom looking out into
the dark world. Through that gate and by
that cot the poachers pass silently, but without
a tremor. The waggoner never calls upon
them to halt.

He knows that they pass by his abode as
regularly as he goes to bed, or the moon rises,
every night. He never demands their pass-
port. Though, apparently, such mild-looking
fellows, he knows right well what murderous
rascals they can be when their plans are crossed
and their business interfered with.

Moreover, he has a fair respect for his own
skin, and no consuming desire to be beaten, or
stoned, or, if needs be—shot. In the daytime he
is even upon nodding terms with the poachers,
and not averse to an occasional rabbit himself,
when it is left upon his doorstep, as the price
paid for his lethargy and silence.

This corruption of the peasant by the town
poacher is a true and lamentable fact. It
must necessarily be so, to a certain extent,
in some neighbourhoods. Many peasants are
poachers at heart. Advanced political teaching
has made them so. If it were not for the fear
of being caught in the act, or otherwise found
out, they would poach every night on their
master's land and leave less game for the town
prowlers.

As it is, I have known farm workers run

the risk of detection; the allurement to poach
being so powerful, and their strength to resist
it so weak. It is not surprising, therefore, that
some Strephons are willing to accept presents
from poachers, rather than run the risk of
detection themselves, as the reward of their
silence in regard to the nightly goings-on of
the town poachers.

❦ ❦ ❦

**The
Sheep
at
Night**
THE crew passed the waggoner's
cottage with merely a side-
long glance at it. The lambs
—long since weaned from the ewes, and now
well-grown in meat, bone and fleece—were
lying about on the hill in knots and heaps. A
few of them rose, looking much bewildered
at the intrusion of the poachers. All of them
shuffled their woolly sides together—frightened
at the mysterious movements of the intruders.

But they had no need to fear. Sheep-steal-
ing is no longer a fashionable branch of poaching science. The bulky ovine is not so easy
to dispose of as the small rodent, and the
chance of detection is ten times greater. A

F

poacher with his wits about him would sooner
'neck' five hundred rabbits than cut the throat
of one sheep or lamb. The fleecy flocks were
therefore perfectly secure, and need not have
opened a single eye.

Still, the effect of them, as seen from the
declining pathway on the south of the hill, was
eerie in the extreme. In the darkness they had
the appearance of a shivering hill—a hill of
living warts or molecaps. Every one of them
shivered, for the night was not a particularly
balmy one. A few of them rose, and those
which did not made a sort of rolling movement towards their fellows.

This motion seemed to endue the entire hill
with life, and as it heaved and gave forth no
sound (as a mountain in labour), the effect was
of the weirdest kind, though not sufficiently so
to startle the poachers.

Nature's
Strange
Moods
THE poachers see Nature in her
strangest moods, and although
mostly inhabitants of towns,
they are less alarmed than the woodcutter at

the manifestations which night draws from Nature.

The rustic, pure and simple, has a firm faith in the tradition of the wych-elm. He believes that an old witch, or ' 'ooman' as he calls her, inhabits the trunk of that tree. Nay, more, he believes that the tree itself is a woman, with the baneful power of changing her shape as often as she pleases—from a woman to a tree, and back again. The superstitions of the lowlands are still deeply implanted in the mind of the average rustic, whether he lives in a village, in a lonely cot on the waste, or close by a wood.

Ordinary poachers have no such leaning towards belief in the supernatural. Their lives have never been tinctured with aught but the severely practical. Not one of those poachers now in the grass lane leading to the close on the north side of the Red House Farm, and passing not far from a wych-elm, would, I believe, be afraid if the trunk of that tree were to open and 'the old 'ooman' herself were to come walking out towards them.

Fear is practically unknown to these night birds. The mysterious lapping and moaning of the river near the Rungells—a small, productive spinney for game to the poacher's net—does not in the least disturb them. Yet it splashes and laps and moans with a crying sort of noise, as though an infant were drowning among the roots and tangle of the river's bed.

Again, the sighing of the saplings in the spinney—a sighing which at night-time seems like the agonised outburst of long-pent-up misery—has no power to blanch the poacher's cheek. Even the squeal of the murdered hare, snatched from its litter of young, has not the power to do it. And if anything could, surely it ought to be that heartrending, despairing scream.

It is only the glimmer of the keeper's or the farmer's gun-barrel, when seen close at hand, pointed at the poacher's breast, that causes the springs of fear to well up within him. The thought of Death to the poacher is a sterner Justice than the 'beak' who sits on the county bench.

The Easygoing Farmer  WHEN the poachers are, however, in the spinney close—that slopes off down to the little, gurgling river, where the marsh-mallow and the wild hyacinth border the banks—there is no fear of keepers.

The farmer of the land there is one of those easy-going individuals who will do anything for peace. He is perfectly conversant with the fact that hundreds of rabbits and hares, and an occasional partridge or pheasant, are poached from the land in his occupation ; for he has not infrequently found a forgotten piece of netting in the field, or a wire snare upon a twig in the spinney, as evidence thereof. He has also found the feathers of a partridge, freshly plucked from the body of a bird, lying in a heap by the first stile leading from his farmyard—the poacher's legacy to him for the stuffing of a chair cushion.

But he only looks at the evidence of the nocturnal visit and wrinkles his face into a smile. Peace above all things is his desire.

When he wants a rabbit for himself he knows where to find one. So what is the use of making a bother about the poachers? No use, he thinks. And so the poachers have a free run round the rabbit warrens on his farm.

His fishing, however, he is much more careful about. There are no fish ponds on his land, as there are on his neighbours', where, if the followers of Isaac Walton would leave them alone, there would soon be carp fat enough even for a country parson of the old school. The Red House has pits, but no ponds; and the fishing rights of the farmer lie in the lazy little river which gurgles over a pebbly bed through his fields and meadows on to Brookington—'the gay Brookington' of the rustic.

Sixpence a day is his fee for fishing, and this price he will enforce with much rigour. If he observes a piscator he thinks has not paid, he will turn his cob's head to the river, ride down there with a vigour fast enough for a win in the Farmer's Plate of the annual Brookington Steeplechases, run over a portion of his farm, and demand 'the nimble tanner'

'WELL STOCKED WITH ROACH, PERCH, CHUB AND PIKE.'

By permission of Messrs Eyre & Spottiswoode.

with a severity strangely in contrast with his easy treatment of the nightly poachers.

As the river, however, at that point is well stocked with roach, perch, chub and pike, and an occasional trout, no one ever begrudges him his fee. Some pay it with a smile, and wonder whether he exacts the silver bits only to return them again to the offertory plate of Lynton village church—whither he repairs most Sundays.

✹ ✹ ✹

Spread-ing the Net HE net is now spread out for a hundred yards or more along by the hedge of the spinney. It is most singular to notice how quiet the poachers are. Not a word do they exchange with one another, and yet the temptation to speak under the circumstances must be very great.

Perhaps the coast is not clear. Mayhap the keen ear of the poacher has caught the 'swish, swish' of the game preserver's boots wading through the dew-moistened grass on the other side of the river. Perhaps—and

most likely reason of all—the poacher knows
by the dimpled and undulating look of the
turf in the field—for before entering the
ground the most experienced man amongst
them lay flat upon the earth, level with the
sky line, and looked out over the pastures—
that more rodents than usual are out on the
feeding-ground.

That is why they are so quiet ; so silent
that any intrusive watcher might think those
dim, crouching forms were bodiless and, in
some unearthly way, a special creation of
mysterious Nature. That is why they can
look no way but on the ground, because
they are of the earth earthy. That is why
they cannot lift their eyes to Heaven, where
the top rim of the silver moon is peeping,
orblike, at their proceedings, over the dark
spinney in their rear.

The Lur-
cher's
Satur-
nalia
IT is now that the mysterious
instincts of the lurcher are
called into play. Up till now
the dog has been sitting up on its haunches,

watching out of its dark eyes the preparations for the slaughter of the innocents. Not a sound has that brindled creature— taught by love or fear — given forth to denote that it is alive. It has sat there, gloomy as a gorged raven, until it has seen the last forked twig—pegging the bottom of the net—stuck into the turf.

A low, peculiar, clucking kind of noise is now heard, so faint as to be almost a doubt. It is the poacher's signal to his dog. It is that which the lurcher has been waiting for.

The dark, statue-like thing darts from its position in a shot. Down towards the river it goes, rapidly and noiselessly, to frighten the feeding rodents into the net, on the top cord of which the poacher keeps his finger. The effect is almost magical ; the lurcher is doing his work so well. His serpent - like sliding through the grass has paralysed the quiet nibblers with a great fear. They rush headlong into the net.

Jerk—jerk—jerk !

The poacher knows the signs. Each jerk foretells the doom of a rodent. Before escape is possible, the big hand of the poacher is down upon it, and its neck is broken. A quivering, shivering creature, with an agonised cry strangled in its throat, is thrown down—never to run again.

As jerk follows jerk the heap of murdered rabbits grows in size. The poachers are having a good haul. Yet they utter not a word ; no single cry escapes them. Even the lurcher, worked up to fever heat with excitement, opens not its mouth. It is a strange, weird spectacle — mysterious, uncanny, unearthly, almost devilish.

The dog works like a fiend. With head now erect and now between its legs, it runs here and there wherever it sees a dimple in the grass, and where, by instinct, it knows right well there lies out a furry little coney, or the parent of a family, enjoying a feed of sweet grass which it will never more enjoy.

The dog's tact is remarkable. It is full of cunning. The hideous creature 'doubles' as quickly as the rodent which it chases. It seems to take a perfect pleasure in its work, as, with its tongue lolling far out of its

mouth, it hurries every victim to the net.
And yet, labouring as it must be under the
most intense excitement, it has been so well
taught by its master that it can never be
induced to 'give mouth.'

⚜ ⚜ ⚜

The
Poach-
ers'
Orgie

IN the meantime, while the
lurcher is enjoying his satur-
nalia of power, the poachers
themselves are having an orgie. Their movements are rapid. It seems to the observer
of their actions as if they reserve *all* their
energy for their nightly work. In the daytime they are sluggish, lethargic, indolent,
downright lazy ; they betray no inclination
to do anything but lounge about with a
pipe between their teeth, waiting for the
day to die.

At night they are new men. Mercury
runs in their veins. Then there is more life
in their finger tips than in the whole of their
bodies during the day. And they need it—
the rush of rabbits is so strong. There is

so much murder to be done. With the same instinct as that animating their dog, they do it without a word. Only a whispered curse ever escapes them; and that is only when one of them has caught a hare, and fails to strangle its child-like scream quick enough.

Their work in the spinney close is now over. Thanks to the ability of their dog and the cunning of their own hands, almost every rodent on the feeding-ground but a few minutes ago now lies lifeless in a heap beside each poacher. Some of them are still shivering and quivering in their death tremors; never to rise again to that full flush of glorious life of which the poacher has bereft them.

To the person of tender heart who intensely loves all creation, it is a piteous sight. The big, round, frightened eyes of the killed creatures would awaken remorse in any heart but the poacher's. *He* has no heart where business is concerned, and only looks with gladness upon the heaps before him, and estimates the price they will fetch.

The
Home-
ward
Jaunt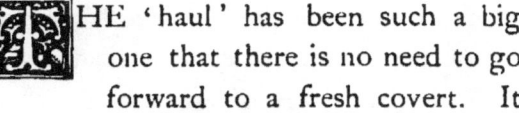HE 'haul' has been such a big one that there is no need to go forward to a fresh covert. It is now only necessary to get the game away with all convenient despatch. On the Red House land this is quite an easy matter, and at this hour. There is no farmer to interrupt, no keeper to waylay, no constable to arrest. The borough police find it difficult to take action owing to legal technicalities; and the county police, having had two or three stiff tussles with the poachers thereabouts, find it most convenient to leave them alone.

And so they pull up their pegs and fold up their nets with as little concern as if they had been sporting on their own land. They assume a virtue and congratulate each other upon a good night's work. They have successfully repudiated their character for idleness which is given them in the daytime.

In complimenting themselves, they have not a word to throw at their dog, without whose services they would have come poorly off. That extraordinary creature, melancholy as ever now the excitement has subsided, walks behind the poachers' heels on the homeward jaunt just as he did on the outward—a silent, shadowy form.

With their bags of game upon their backs, the poachers toil up the golf hills from the Red House, and disappear, moodily, in the gloom of 'the Black Lane.'

The Poacher's Friend

The Poacher's Friend

SCENES OF POACHING LIFE

That night a bairn might understan',
The de'il had business on his han'.

The Poach-er's Faithful Lurcher

THERE goes the dark-brindled lurcher,
tiger-striped, sharp-eyed and thin,
Alongside his gloomy master, who
battles with life, but can't win;
Sour-looking, slippery brute, with long-eared
head bent down,
A dog to make one shudder, but as faithful as any in
town.

A sore-sided beggar is he, for the poacher's all love and
kicks,
And the serpent-like, sliding lurcher has had kisses and
boots and sticks;
But he looks from between the legs of the man who has
made him bend,
And by an invisible thread of love he becomes the
poacher's friend.

The love of a brindled lurcher that exists in the sties and
stews,
Is a stronger love than a poacher has when his pal is in for
a bruise;

G

A poacher's butties will cut and run, and carry the nets
and go,
But a lurcher will stand by his master and share his last
hour of woe.

When the land is dark and the partridge is left in peace
for a night,
And the song-birds fly to the south by the aid of the pale
moonlight;
'Tis then that the creeping poacher into rabbit-land
silently steals,
A poacher with sticks and snares and stones, and a brindled
cur at his heels.

Work in the lonely night-time is work that the poacher
loves,
Kneeling down and setting his snares beneath the nest of
the doves;
But the plaint of the milk-white woodling charms not the
poacher's ear,
The squeal of the hare and rabbit to Ishmael's heart is
dear.

When the silvery bells of the village chime, that softens
the souls of men,
Float on the early autumn air the darkened hour of ten,
A shadow as dark as the poacher's crime, stalks lengthening
into the field;
' 'Tis the keeper!' the poacher thinks, and vows that to
him he will not yield.

Then the lurcher, with long ears cocked and tiger-striped
body bent,
Is ready to fly at the comer's throat even before he is
sent;

For a lurcher, a dog, a cur—sworn at and kicked in the
stews—
Has a stronger love than a poacher has when his master is
in for a bruise.

Eyes glittering like molten fire, a body all writhing and
limp,
Snake-like crawling along the ground—a sort of canine
imp ;
Straight leaps the faithful lurcher at the breast of the
coming man—
A lurcher, heedless of sticks and stones, careless of kick
or ban.

A shot—an oath—a thud, and down to the ground one
falls !
A poacher has found an ending at last to his nightly
brawls ;
The shots have pierced his side—gone clean through him
—taken his breath;
He is caught in the snarer's net—and the poacher is cast
for death.

But where is the hungry lurcher—a dark thing whining
around,
Sniffing and licking at something that stretches itself on
the ground?
There lies the hand that smote him, the foot that never
was known to spare,
But the lurcher remembers nothing save that his master
lies bleeding there.

When the moon with its sickly glimmer shone on the
poacher's face,
There sat the ugly lurcher, glued to the ghastly place;

A miserable lurcher whining and moaning, licking his
    master's lips,
The lips that will never call him again—from which the
    blood-spot drips.

And all through the darkling hours, when no craven
    poacher came nigh,
The lurcher sat by the dying man, and looked into his
    filming eye ;
A friend to the erring soul as he battled his breath away,
They found him stretched at his master's feet in the light
    of the opening day.

The History of Brookington

THE Brookington in which 'the King' was born, and followed, first, the occupation of honest carpenter, and second, the 'profession' of dishonest poacher, was one of those towns, or rather villages, which spring up into notice with the rapidity of a mushroom's growth.

Not a century ago—as the President of the Warwickshire Natural History and Archæological Society would inform the hunter after antiquity—Brookington was but a small village of thirty houses, all thatched with straw, and forming the roof-trees to a little colony of less than one hundred people.

At that time its chief recommendation to the notice of posterity was the somewhat vague supposition that Shakespeare halted at Brookington, for the purpose of refreshing his inner man at the sign of 'the Black Dog,' when on that memorable tramp to Babylon to seek fame and fortune; which he duly found and duly brought back with him to Stratford-on-Avon.

Whether or not the immortal playwright did make Brookington a sort of half‑way house on his coachless journey to London, the fact remains that the supposition that he did produced no radical or volcanic change in the condition of Arcadian Brookington for two or three centuries. The two or three farmers resident there in the days when George the Third was king turned over their land and set their seeds and grain. Strephon went out to field labour, and Phyllis worked at her spinning-wheel or in the dairy.

Then they died comfortably, at a good old age, and were comfortably buried under the daisies in the quaint little graveyard.

That is all the history and all the romance

of ancient Brookington. The name of Shakespeare, therefore, in this case did not prove a great attraction.

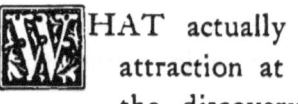

The Saline Springs HAT actually did serve as an attraction at Brookington was the discovery, in 1808, of a spring of saline water, the quaffing of which was supposed to act like magic upon the painful and disordered bodies of poor humanity.

It certainly acted like magic in the reformation of the obscure and quaint little village, which at that time had never been disturbed by the sound of a coach horn. The place was too sequestered and the roads too dangerous at that time for a coach to enter upon. The saline waters, however, revolutionised everything in the slowly-passing life of leafy Brookington.

In a short space of time the roads were metamorphosed into streets, and the village into a town; the peasants began to die off one by one, and in their place came dukes and duchesses, lords, ladies and gentlemen, and the parasitic following from big towns and cities.

The beautiful, quiet, sylvan village, with all its quaint and peaceful associations which the thoughtful mind loves to contemplate, was killed easily by the inroads of modern civilisation; and the sequestered hamlet of Brookington, with astonishing quickness, became a fashionable Spa, where everybody of note rose early in the morning and walked sharply to the wells, with little glass tumblers and goblets in their hands, from which they sipped the prescribed quantity of saline as a cure for all the ills that flesh is heir to.

A river, very lazy, and not particularly clean, sweet, or pretty, ran right through the middle of the old hamlet; so that when Brookington expanded, consequent upon the discovery of the magic springs, there became two towns as it were—one on the north and one on the south side of the river.

The Upper Town

FOR some years the south side of the town was the most fashionable, but the north was more breezy, more elevated, and more thickly studded

with trees.   Moreover, it was closer to the
coverts of Squire Newbold, where foxes were
attentively nursed for the future pleasure of
incoming sportsmen.   So ever-varying fashion
soon removed its dovecotes from the south of
Brookington, where the saline wells were, to
the upper reaches of the town, where health,
beauty and recreation were to be had in larger
quantities.

As the laws of humanity do not permit any
section of humanity to isolate itself from the
other sections—for every class of society in
some measure depends upon each other—the
poor went to live in the north of Brookington,
as well as the rich.   In that day, too, the
builder of the architecture seemed to strive,
not so much after elegance and healthfulness,
as to erect as many dwellings as possible upon
the smallest slice of ground.

Thus, in north Brookington there were im-
posing mansions in the front of the streets, and
networks of narrow courts and alleys at the
back, in which the breath of Heaven, or the
light of day, could rarely penetrate.   It was a
palpable and sometimes a melancholy instance

of the rich and the poor meeting together ; for
the Brookington rich were very rich, and the
Brookington poor were very poor.

Clinging to the very outskirts of the Newbold estates was a fairly large colony of courts,
alleys, passages and slums, in which the dwellings were especially erected for 'the poor';
and in the erection of which several well-known
demons of social life, such as bad ventilation,
bad light, bad drainage and bad material played
a leading part.   In the cottage at the end of one
of these slums lived Jack Compton, familiarly
known as 'the King of the Poachers.'

*   *   *

 The
King's
'Dig-
gings'
THIS cottage, or 'diggings' as
Compton called it, was admir-
ably suited to the life which
he led.   It was cheap—being only two shillings
and sixpence a week.   It was also, in his estima-
tion, very 'snug'—fixed as it was at the end
of a narrow passage which led to rows of stables
and cow-sheds, and no other human habitations.

And what was more in its favour to Jack
Compton, was the fact that the mouth of the

passage exactly fronted 'the Ivy Tree.' For,
as the poacher stood at the door of his hut,
smoking his pipe, he could see the open door
of the tavern ; could observe who entered the
dingy haunt ; and—sweetest music in a tippler's
ear—he could hear the jingling glasses and the
coarse, ribald songs and speeches of his crew of
butties that assembled there.

To him, therefore, his 'diggings' were well
placed ; and he would march over the refuse-
strewn floor of the passage to his wretched
domicile with as much recklessness and scorn
of taste as used to characterise him in the days
when he lived in a pretty, bow-windowed house
in one of the front streets.

The effluvium from the horse-boxes and
cow-sheds—which were not cleansed out as
often as they should have been—had no effect
upon *his* olfactory organs ; and within *his*
system, at least, the fearful atmosphere of the
place seemed powerless to breed that disease
which had long been setting its hated marks
upon the pale face of his wife—once a pretty
young woman with a bright face and a dimpled
figure ; but now, owing to the treatment of

her 'lord and master,' an object disagreeable
even to the eyes of him who had made her so.

~ ~ ~

 King
and
Friend
TO-DAY 'the King' is sitting
before the well-polished little
fire - grate — for though her
earnings are very small and she is very poorly
in health, Mary Compton never permits the
hovel to go dirty—waiting for the day to die
and the night with its darkness to cloud on.

He is killing time with the aid of a quart
pot of 'four ale,' a clay pipe, and, as it seems,
an unlimited supply of black tobacco. He is
as silent as the lurcher dog between his legs,
and rarely looks or speaks to his wife, who is
washing a few clothes in a shadowed corner
of the room—a wearied, jaded woman, passing
a living death each day.

'Drat you, Ty,' thundered the poacher,
suddenly, with a half-drunken voice, as he
kicked the poor lurcher, which, being in
dreamland, was blissfully ignorant of the fact
that he was snoring and disturbing the medita-
tions of his master.

'Get up, you old beggar!' he continued;
'you lazy demon! You've been snoozing and
snoring there all the blessed day. Get up, you
idle snake—do you hear?'

And with his big, hob-nailed boots, this once
kind and humane man kicked the brute again,
till it fairly howled with pain.

The woman looked at her husband, and
dropped her head and sighed, and by a great
effort restrained herself from speaking. She
had often before taken the dog's part, and
just as many times had she been bruised and
cursed for her sympathy. So now she held
her peace.

As for the dog—the dark-brindled, tiger-
striped lurcher—the poor thing bent its form
snake-like to the ground, looked piteously up
to its master's hard, brutal, unrelenting face,
licked the tears from its eyes into its mouth,
crawled round the room once or twice, and
slunk once more between the ruffian's legs.

Between this sad-looking, lean and slippery
brute, and Jack Compton, there seemed a
strange tie, which the deeply-studied psycho-
logist would find a difficulty in explaining.

A beaten cur rarely loves the hand that
beats it. In the human creation blows inspire
hatred and a desire for vengeance, rather than
love and a wish to befriend. How then
should a lurcher, a dog, a cur, a creature with
small reasoning power, who has been sworn
at and kicked in the stews until there is not
a painless piece of flesh upon its body—how
can such a victim of violence be animated with
aught but hatred for his grim and ghoulish
oppressor?

Yet 'Tyrant,' or 'Ty,' as he was called—
the poacher's lurcher—seemed to be joined by
an invisible thread of love to his gross and
brutish master, who not only bruised and
broke his limbs, but half-starved him as
well.

He would writhe and bend his narrow body
down to the ground to receive the smiting.
He would go into a corner of the room for
a few minutes, and stare at his oppressor with
moist eyes. Then the magnetic influence of
the invisible love-thread would operate upon
the feelings of the dog, and he would crawl
back again between the hob-nailed boots, and

stretch himself out comfortably upon the hearthstone.

The man said he loved the dog, and perhaps he did, with that coarse animal passion with which a full-blooded Russian loves the woman whose tender flesh he flays with a horsewhip.

At times, indeed, when the man was more dominant than the beast in Jack Compton—truly a fine and ancient name to drag in the mire of a poacher's career—he would play with the ugly lurcher for hours; would kiss the creature's sharp nose; rub him behind the ears; call him a good, clever dog; and favour him with the remains of the last poached rabbit. But the dog's life was not a happy one, in spite of these periods of endearment. He received more kicks than kisses; less love and less food than so faithful a creature deserved.

Charms of Scenery

EVERY night when the darkness came down, 'the King' and his butties stealthily crept from the elegant 'diggings' at the top of the passage fronting 'the Ivy Tree,' and stole off

eastward—with their nets, their sticks, their
stones and their lurcher—in the direction of
the Red House Farm. If the poachers had
poor sport there, they would advance to
grounds adjoining, where they always reckoned
upon making a 'good haul.' The Red House
Farm, however, as a poacher's hunting ground,
was considered one of the best in Warwickshire, and had the advantage of being free from
gamekeepers.

It was to this ground that 'the King,' his
two butties, 'the Squire' and 'the Parson,' and
the patient, silent lurcher crept off on the night
of which this sketch is to treat.

Warwickshire has been called 'the heart of
England' in its gentle beauty, and no doubt it
justifies the description of the poet Drayton.
There there is no grand scenery to draw
expressions of wonder to the lips of the rambler.
No beetling crags aspiring to reach the clouds,
and seeming, to the awed gazer, as though a
strong breath from Boreas would send them
shattering and crashing into the deeps below.
No snowy waterfalls which appear to rise in the
white clouds and come splashing down to the

parched and arid earth, making the solitudes echo with a weird and beautiful rhythm.

Charms and wonders like these are not indigenous to the soil of Warwickshire, and the searcher for beauty there must be prepared to find it in a more gentle, smooth, and, it might with truth be added, a lovelier form. For the ruggedness and grandeur of Nature inspire awe rather than delight, and Warwickshire—in that part where Brookington is situated—inspires delight all the year round, and especially at night.

At night when the red sun has gone to his evening rest in the western sky, and the moon has risen to lighten somewhat the heart of many a cheerless labourer, plodding with leaden feet to his little, white-washed home from his daily work in the fields.

When, from the misty minds of these some-what awkward and dilapidated Strephons— minds, perhaps, clouded with the potations of stale beer which they have been drinking in the snug bar-parlour of 'the White Lion' or 'the George and Dragon'—the crisp night wind blows away some of the cobwebs.

When the town loafers, with cunning faces and undersized figures, are lured abroad late to catch the peacefully browsing rodents, or to creep, like mean murderers, upon the retiring pheasants, who are sleeping the sleep of the beautiful and virtuous, each on its own twig, in the spinnies and the woods.

When the whole earth, like a scarcely convalescent invalid, covers itself with a cloudy mantle, and appears to the eye that beholds it a fresh, a new, and a beautiful creation, made by the hand of the Giver of all Good for the benefit and enjoyment of all mankind—the rich, the poor, the humble, the proud.

The Poach-er's Wife

THOUGHTS of the beauty of Nature's world, however, do not trouble the minds of men bent upon desperate enterprises, and they did not one whit disturb the minds of Jack Compton and his companions.

The former, before he started from his 'diggings,' had kissed his wife, a most unusual thing for a man to do who was often pommelling

her with his fists. It was showing the same kind
of love to Mary as he showed to his dog—a kiss
to-night and a kick to-morrow. At the same
time the kiss had a marked effect upon his wife,
who had become inured to curses and blows
rather than kind words and kisses, and if Jack
Compton himself had been asked why he kissed
his wife that night so strangely and spontane-
ously, he could not have answered the question
to his own satisfaction.

'Good night, Poll, my lass,' he said, as he
put a hundred yards of netting into the big
'poacher's pocket' in the inside of his slouch
coat. 'Kiss the crew of kiddies for me, and
take that for yourself,' kissing her. 'Go to
bed now. I sha'n't be home till latish.'

'The King' stumbled out of the hovel,
slammed the door behind him, and was gone
—with his lurcher between his heels—on his
wild and, it might be, desperate errand.

Poor Poll, perplexed and bewildered, opened
the door noiselessly, gazed after him until she
saw him turn the corner and fade from her
sight. Then she shut and catched the door,
dropped into a chair, and gave way to those

tears which seem to be such a comfort to
women who have bad and cruel husbands.

She wondered why Jack had kissed her.
And the fact that he had was just sufficient to
make her cry. For months now he had gone
out without saying where he was going—
though Poll knew pretty well where his haunts
were—or when he should be back ; and now he
had kissed her and bidden her ' Good-night.'

It seemed to her surprised senses as if the old
times had returned, those old days of respect-
ability and comfort, when Jack, who had sworn
to love, honour and cherish her, did, in a
measure, fulfil his nuptial vow. Oh ! how
happy the woman was ! She seemed to see the
dawn of coming joy ; and she went, a little
later, up the creaking stairs to bed, with the
bright torch of Hope flaming in her heart.

A Rural Night Scene MEANTIME Jack Compton, his
butties and his lurcher, moved
like dumb spectres through
the dark fields towards the Red House Farm.
Not a word was spoken by the three men.

Their plans were all prepared, and the dog—
with that strange instinct peculiar to lurchers,
who seem to have the brains of human beings
for depth in cunning—crawled behind their legs
with something of the goblin about it.

Crossing a somewhat lofty and pleasant hill—
on the western side of which the golfer drives
his merry ball—which in the daytime afforded
a fine playground for the children of upper
Brookington, the mysterious quartette—three
men and the dog—skirted a quaint little pool,
where a society of frogs and natterjacks were
located and were croaking a dismal chorus;
thence they passed through a clapgate, noise-
less as shadows, into a narrow, winding lane,
on each side of which there grew a row of
those tall elms for which Warwickshire has
long been noted.

A slight wind had sprung up, and as the
poachers and the dog crept stealthily along by
the hedge, the trees on each side of the lane
seemed to sigh and bend forward, as if to
question the intruders concerning their ghostly
errand.

Of this strange proceeding of Nature the

poachers took no heed. They shambled
silently on down the lane, over a field of
barren land, then through a sort of mimic
ravine—from the elevated sides of which the
light-sleeping sheep could be dimly seen
shuffling about at the intrusion—until they
reached a five-barred gate, which led to the
most productive rabbit close on the Red
House Farm.

In the daytime the close over which 'the
King of the Poachers' and his familiars spread
their nets afforded a pretty sight to the
searcher after country pleasures and earthly
quiet. On the south side it sloped gently
down to where the puny stream of water,
which passed through Brookington, grew
smaller and smaller, until it became the tiniest
of brooklets, in which the oxen used to stand
for hours, cooling themselves, on a bright,
warm summer's day.

Over the little runnel some two or three
fields revealed that flat yet satisfying beauty
for which that part of Warwickshire is so well
known. A little further on could be seen,
flashing white against the sky, the improved

and renovated church of Redford.   Its new
white walls broke the line of continuity between
them and the old square tower, whose stone
had been darkened by the weather of two
centuries, but which now stood out almost as
strong and sound as the material just added.

The north side of the poacher's hunting
ground was high land, running to the village
of Cuddington, and thickly studded with
spinnies and little woods, from which the
rodents came in hundreds to the lower feed-
ing-grounds.

This scene, in which 'the King' and his
butties moved about like objects foreign to its
beauty and quietude, was always charming in
the daylight ; and on certain nights, when the
moon was flooding the land with silver sheen,
it was pleasant to walk as far into the core of
Nature's heart as the Red House Farm.   But
on a dark night, when there is no moon and
scarcely a star to be seen with the naked eye,
the spot is not so charming.

In fact, on the night in question, this portion
of the landscape had a rather weird and uncanny
look about it, which in some breasts would

have inspired a feeling of awe. The trees in
the spinney on the north side seemed like a
battalion of county justices, with beards of
formal cut, all arrayed in order there to deal
out summary judgment to breakers of the game
laws ; and the silvery bells of the village chime
pealing from Redford church tower should have
sounded in the poachers' ears as a voice warning
them of the danger into which they were wil-
fully entering.

But reflection, as a rule, is not the poacher's
strong point, and it was not the strong point
of Jack Compton and his pals. They thought
only of 'the big haul' which they were going
to make ; and although they spoke no word
to each other, they were brimming over with
suppressed excitement.

All along by the frowning spinney on the
north side of the close the crouching men
pegged down their nets. Then—without being
told—the serpent-like, sliding lurcher, with the
instinct of a human being, ran off down the
meadow like a creature of an eerie world, to
frighten the feeding rodents into the net spread
out for their destruction.

 The Keeper

IN a few minutes the net shook with a vigorous shaking. Not with the effect of a mass of rabbits or hares leaping into it—an effect so well known to the habitual poacher—but with a bold, tight tug, as though some heavy weight had fallen into the snare.

Jack Compton and his mates knew there must be something wrong. They therefore laid their bodies flat upon the dewy grass, and looked towards the western sky, where the hedges were low, and from which part of the net they knew the tugging had come.

There, on the background of the sky, they could see a tall figure loom up from the turf, upon which it had evidently been thrown by its feet having been caught in the net. It was the figure of a man, gaunt and dark ; a shadow as dark as the poachers' crime, and it stalked lengthening into the field — like a nocturnal Nemesis upon the track of the law-breakers.

''Tis the keeper !' the men instinctively muttered as they rose up from their crouching

positions, vowing, by dumb signs, that they
would not yield.

And the dog, the lurcher, that had been
beaten and bruised, and sworn at and kicked
in the stews, also came up, crawling upon its
belly, with its long ears cocked and its eyes
glittering like molten fire. Even this grovel-
ling creature—looking in the gloom like the
offspring of a cross between a dog and a snake
—had a love for the hand that smote it. It
scented danger, and it was ready to risk its life
for the life of its unworthy and brutal master.

**The
Fallen
King**   EEDLESS of sticks and stones,
careless of kick or curse, the
dark - brindled, tiger - striped
lurcher leaped straight at the breast of the
coming man, and that brought things to a
crisis.

A shot—an oath—a thud; and one of the
poachers went down!

Then all was silence, save for the whining
and sniffing of the lurcher, licking the face
of a figure lying prostrate upon the grass.

The mysterious visitant with the gun, who had fallen into the net over the pegs, and had —doubtless, in his dread of being in the midst of a gang of desperate men—discharged his gun, was nowhere to be seen. He had disappeared as strangely as he had come.

Meantime fright had seized upon the poachers, most of whom are arrant cowards at heart. The disabled man lay upon the ground, moaning piteously, while the pair of able ruffians ripped up the pegs and nets, and cut out of the close as fast as their legs and the darkness would allow them, leaving their comrade on the field weltering in his blood.

And that comrade was Jack Compton, 'the King of the Poachers.'

The shots from the gun had pierced his side, gone clean through him, taken his breath. He was caught in the snarer's net, and Jack Compton, the renegade from a life of honesty, decency and sobriety, was cast for death.

The King's Friend

BUT Jack was not left alone to die, though his butties had cut and run, fearful for the safety of their own hides. The hungry dog was there, the lurcher whom Jack, in his moments of brutality, had taken a malicious joy in kicking and cursing. *He* would not leave the dying 'King' if the 'King's' human friends would. So he stayed there, like a sentinel, watching his master ebbing his breath away.

It was a strange and piteous sight as the night drew on and the moon rose, casting a sickly glimmer through the trees upon the face of the fallen man.

To any eye but the filming eye of the poacher, and the all-seeing eye of God, that sight was at once strange, weird and wonderful. The man lying there, slowly and surely dying; the dog, raven-like, and yet Christian-like, sitting by him, whining and moaning, and ever and anon licking the blood-spots from his master's lips—lips that would never call him again on this earth.

There were the feet that had kicked the dog; there were the fists that smote him, powerless now to do the creature any hurt. But the lurcher remembered no pains, only the poacher's pale forehead kissed. And all through the darkling hours the dog sat there. No craven poacher came, or roused gamekeeper. Only the man and the dog, 'the King' dying; the dog acting as friend to the erring soul, and comforting him with his dumb love and sorrow.

What a picture of unselfish devotion! Where could be found such a counterpart, even among the human family, who are exhorted to 'love one another?'

When the dim light of morning appeared, two labourers, going out to field work, crossed the close, and found the man and dog still there. The man was dead, stiff and stark; the lurcher was glued to the ghastly place, and would not leave till the body of 'the King' was carried to the nearest inn.

Even then he followed with downcast head and drooping tail as chief mourner.

The Two Shepherds

The Two Shepherds

And every shepherd tells his tale
Under the hawthorn in the dale.
Milton.

**The
Compn
Farm** HERE are two farms and two shepherds. The farms both lie in the east, snugly planted down in the greenwood between Brookington and Overchurch. The former is a town—'a gay town.' Some dignify it with the name of 'fashion resort,' though what that means only those know who utter it. The latter is a village.

Walking eastward from the promenades of 'gay Brookington,' where the fashion that resorts there idles away its time in looking at the furs and feathers, and the waxen women and boys in the shop windows, until it has no time to even peep at the much more lovely aspect of Nature's face, you come to the end of the town.

127

It is a veritable town's end. There the village begins. But strange to say, the Comyn Farm and the Red House Farm, which is the other farm where the other shepherd is, purely rural as they are, are within the parish of the town.

As you stand at the clapgate, one of those new, modern, creaking engines of iron, more common amid Warwickshire greenery now than in the days when Urbane Holt first became shepherd of the Comyn Farm, you can see the peaked ricks, five or six of them, showing here and there in the openings between the trunks of the trees that mark the limit of the field next to that in which the farm is planted. You can also see the red gables of the farmhouse, and the west end of the buildings, adding colour and variety to the scene.

Urbane Holt. Shepherd SOMETIMES if you pass through the clapgate, and walk along a gravel path to the second clapgate—made in barbarous iron like the first

—sometimes, I say, if you lean thereon, admiring the purely rural aspect of the scene, you may see a figure clothed in dirty white come out of the gate of the rickyard, with a dog behind him—sometimes with two dogs, parent and child, both of the collie breed.

That is Urbane Holt, the shepherd.

If I said that, in the distance, when the morning is misty, as the mornings often are in the autumn of the year, Urbane looked more like the large goose of the Comyn Farm flock than like a man, it would not be an unapt description of this head servant of the farm. At a long range—because Urbane was short in stature and wore a coat of a colour between drab and white, and because, moreover, he had a waddling gait, owing to the bulk of flesh with which he was clothed—he really looked remarkably goose-like.

Should a person unacquainted with the natural history of the landscape in this neighbourhood ever make the mistake of likening Urbane Holt to a goose when seeing him trundling his body through the long grass from the rickyard, there would be ample

I

excuse for the error. That was the foraging ground for the flock of geese.

Urbane Holt was, to use his own words, 'not a perticklar man.' That is to say, he was not a rigid stickler for work in his own department. He was a thoroughly good shepherd, and trustworthy withal; in fact, he is so now, for at the date of this sketch he is still the head-servant of the Comyn Farm. He loved the cows, the sheep, the lambs and the little he-goat with almost a woman's affection; but albeit shepherding was his real profession, he was 'not a perticklar man' when a hand was wanted to do a share of farm work in any other branch.

There never was a day when he did not do something apart from shepherding. His wide, happy-looking face, with a sort of sanctified glow spreading all over it—for Urbane was deeply impregnated with religious feeling, being, while he was a villager and lived at Overchurch, a good and fervent 'Methody,' and, now that he had come to live at Brookington, attached to the Salvation Army—was to be seen everywhere, thrusting its sunshine into every scene.

'Should ye be able to give us a lift with the oats to-day, Urbane?' his master, Mr Falcon, would say, in that soft and kindly way which always commanded an answer in the affirmative. 'George is gone to Brookington with the lambs.'

'Yea, maister,' Urbane would reply. 'I be not a perticklar man, an' I perceives as the wuts do want cuttin'. I'll raggle on a bit in the One Acre, an' then come up. A good blade, maister, pleese, an' a good whetstun.'

These were always the demands of Urbane when asked to help in the cornfield, and they were always complied with with a smile; for the shepherd was a man generally liked, and he had a strong will and a strong arm, and knew how to use both when necessary, without a word of complaint.

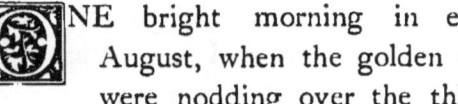

Among Tbe Oats ONE bright morning in early August, when the golden oats were nodding over the thick-set hedge at each passer-by, I took the path

northward from the Comyn Farm to the Red
House.   That is my favourite way.   There
you can see Nature's face and hear Nature's
voice, mingled with no harsh or discordant
noises, such as are sometimes heard in the
streets of gay Brookington.

Few people ever go that way, for I alone
seem to have discovered its beauty out of all
the Brookington idlers who loiter on the
Parade every afternoon, and admire that waxen
woman in the fashionable perruquier's—the one
with the blonde hair done up in the latest
Parisian design.

As I neared the crown of the land and could
begin to look down into the coombe-like hollow
in which the Red House Farm is seated, I
heard a swish, swish, swishing sort of noise,
something like the sound emitted from a
labourer in corduroys when his knees knock
together.   There was the same symmetry of
sound and the same sweeping motion.

On coming to a gap in the hedge of the
western fence, there I saw Urbane Holt, the
shepherd of the Comyn Farm, stripped to his
shirt (for the day was an extraordinarily hot

one) with his brown, sinewy arms bared to the
shoulder, and a straw hat, with a very large brim
to keep the sun out of his eyes, upon his head ;
there I saw him, bowing with graceful sweeps,
and making the ranks of oats fall before him
like soldiers before a deadly discharge of Maxim
guns.

'So you are harvesting, Urbane?' I said,
when I came to the gap.

I had known the shepherd for some time.
He 'looked arter' the fishing as well as the
cattle, and had introduced me to the holes where
the big fish lay, along the banks of the willow-
fringed river.

'Yea,' he replied. 'Maister axed me to lend
a 'and, an' I be not a perticklar man, you know,
when there's summat to be done. The wuts
were ripe for the blade, d'yer see, an' when
things be ripe 'tis time to begin on 'em.'

The
Rus-
tic's
Assur-
ance
WHEREAT he set the handle of
his scythe upon the ground,
and drew out a whetstone from
a pouch at his side and gave his blade a good

whetting. They had a corn-cutting machine at
the Farm, and Urbane preceded it by mowing a
groove all round the field near the hedge, the
better for the machine to do its work ; and in
cutting the way he always used a scythe instead
of a sickle, as one sweep of the former blade
cut the groove the exact width required for
the passage of the two horses yoked to the
machine.

Then he laid his scythe down gently on the
fallen grain, wiped the sweat from his brow
with a red and white cotton handkerchief, and
walked to where his smock lay in a huddled
heap by the hedge. From the crown of the
heap he took a flag-basket, and a quart tin
bottle with a narrow neck, topped with a
cork.

At first when I saw Urbane Holt lay down
his scythe and put his whetstone in the sheath
at his side, I rather marvelled as to what he
was about to do. When I beheld him produce
the flag-basket and the tin bottle I no longer
wondered.

Urbane was about to partake of his luncheon.

Warwickshire peasants are not gifted with

many forms of shyness. In their uncultured
and simple way they stand upon no ceremony.
Without a particle of book-learning, and with
but an imperfect knowledge of the ethics of
what are known as 'good manners,' the rustics
are the possessors of as much assurance as the
most accomplished Richard Dazzle of Mayfair.

Urbane Holt, the shepherd of the Comyn
Farm, was troubled with no refined misgivings
as to the good manners of feeding before a com-
parative stranger. He would not mind stretch-
his mouth to the fullest limit even before a
king, when it was to receive a miniature brick
of home-made bread, and another brick, equal
in size, of his home-fed bacon—these to be
followed by a long draught of his wife's
home-made herb beer, with a foamy head
upon it.

No; no superfine thoughts of this description
interfered with the shepherd's enjoyment of his
homely luncheon. He sat upon his smock with
a stout buckthorn bush to lean against, and,
spreading his kerchief over his knees, did ample
justice to the contents of the flag-basket and the
tin bottle.

In Russet Mantle Clad T was a repast to envy. The rustic partook of it with such zest, and was surrounded with accessories so much more beautiful than are to be found in the most sumptuous dining-rooms —the glories of Nature, lavishly arranged by her own hand.

Before him was the waving grain, shimmering under the glossy morning sun like a sea of molten gold. Beyond, crowning the golden field, rose the green hill which formed a spur of the semi-circular range, which extended from there as far as the Red House Farm— making the red-peaked building appear as though embedded in a deep coombe. The hedge that bounded the hill was still richly decorated with red and white dog-roses and creamy woodbine blossom.

On the south of the lunching shepherd, the land ran in a gentle slope down to the river; and when he turned his eyes that way, he could see his lambs and sheep and young bullocks browsing in the meadow, and could also espy the tops of the bordering willows, whose leaves shone silvery white as the sun's rays fell upon them ; while at his very feet the red poppy and the white moon daisy lent a gaudy variation to the other hues by which he was encircled.

The scene was one of perfect rural happiness, and the shepherd was in harmony with the scene. He was part of it ; he grew with it ; he was inseparable from it.

As I gazed upon his bright, unclouded face, always wearing a smile, and looking as if nothing in the world could ever make it change, I could not help contrasting it with the face of the other shepherd, Amos Oats of the Red House Farm, whose face was harrowed with wrinkles and had not a gleam of sunshine upon it.

☙ ☙ ☙

Rustic Collo- que I COULD not forbear to note, too, how the heart of Urbane seemed to be taken up with his work and the immediate things he was doing, whereas, as I called to mind, the heart of Amos seemed to be in another sphere than that in which he lived and moved and had his being.

Nothing more widely different, I thought,

than the faces of those two shepherds—one all
sunshine, the other overcast with gloom and
despair.

'You appear to be a man who enjoys life,
Urbane?' I said, after I had noted, with great
interest, the rustic's scorn of ceremony.

'Why shunna I?' he replied, with his mouth
full of home-made bread and home-fed bacon.
'I works hard, 'cause I be not a perticklar man
as regards what I does, though shepherding o'
course is my proper work, an' I enjoys myself
accordingly. 'Tain't no child's play, I can tell
thee, to be shepherd on this farm. It's different
to that yon' (pointing with his open pocket-
knife to the Red House Farm). 'There's no
stock theer, while I've got above two hundred
sheep and lambs, fifty milking cows, and about
twenty-five bullocks to see arter.

'You see that medder yon?' he said, filling
his mouth again, and pointing with his knife to
a meadow in the east corner of the landscape,
right away in the direction of Redford village.
'We call that One Acre Medder 'cause its just
one acre big. Well, I tek my fifty milkers
down theer every morning, an' fetches 'em

back every evenin'. A tidy jaunt 'tis, too, I reckon, from the farm. But I donna mind. I be not a perticklar man, and, thank God ! I be sound in wind an' limb, as saying is.'

'And you never feel down in the dumps, Urbane ? ' I suggested, knowing full well that the shepherd never did, but anxious to lead up to the melancholy Amos.

' In the dumps ? ' he repeated, with a merry laugh. 'Not me. Not for my mother's son. Why, mister, my mother's nigh on eighty year old, an' her's as merry as may be now. I hanna ever seed her in the dumps, an' I hanna ever seed myself in 'em neyther. It's un-accountable how folks can get i' that way, wi' such a gladsome sky overhead and such a fruit-ful earth beneath 'em. But I suppose 'em canna 'elp it. 'Tis as was to be, I guess. 'Tis sad, 'owever, for folks to be born so, so 'tis, an' I donna care who the man is as says it inna.'

, 'Your neighbour "Amos " wants some of your cheerfulness,' I said.

Urbane looked at me hard with a meaning twinkle in his quick eyes, as much as to say,

'Theer's summat wrong theer,' and throwing up his chin at the risk of biting his tongue, for his mouth was crammed full of food, and he might easily have mistaken his tongue for the bacon, he gave vent to a kind of 'cluck, cluck,' depreciative rather than appreciative of the condition of Amos.

He also shook his head in a peculiar manner ; the language of it being, 'Ah ! I know summat, if I'd a mind to tell.'

It was like the voluntary to the church service, the prelude to the performance, the prologue to the play ; or, more to the point still, it was like his scythe to the corn-cutter.

'I be sorry for Shepherd Armos,' he said. 'There's no call to say naught about the farm, though that 'ud give me the blues any day o' the week ; such an unked place as it be, wi' scarcely a cow's head on't, and the vittles, as I hear, no better nor 'em should be. But I baint sorry for Shepherd Armos only for that. 'Twere that gel o' hisen as did it, you know, an' 'appen I should 'ave been the same as Ame be if that there misfortin 'ad come to me.'

 A Pastoral Drama

RBANE'S face had now put on a serious look, a kind of melancholy in its babyhood, and as he ate his luncheon more deliberately, pausing between each munch, I could see that something out of the ordinary way was working in his thoughts.

'What misfortune was that, Urbane?' I hazarded.

He took a good long pull at the tin bottle of herb beer, rose from his sitting posture, having finished his bread and bacon, took up his scythe again and gave the golden oats one graceful sweep round, laying a heap of slender stalks prostrate at his feet. Then he set the scythe down again and leant upon the handle.

'His gel drunded hersel' in the pool below the hill yon. Ah! my stars and constellations, Rose were the prettiest gel as ever I clapt eyes on. She were flighty, though, like all uncommon pretty gels be, an' seems to 'ave gone out on the right way wi' some dandified feller from Brookington.

'Anyway, one night when it were pitch dark

and her conscience were plaguing her terrible,
she drund hersel' in that pool as I tells thee
on ; an' Armos fund her theer, an' pulled her
outen, but 'twere too late, poor lass ! Hey, she
wheer uncommon preety, though—uncommon.'

'And that has made him melancholy ! No
wonder,' I said.

'Well, you see, she were his only gel—his
only child, in fact, an' he took it very sadly.
That were ten year agoo come Martimas Day—
I mind the time 'cause it were the loveliest
weather I ever seed in November—an' Shepherd
Armos 'ave never bin the same mon sin then.
He were as merry as a cock pigeon afore that
come on him. Poor Armos ! I be sorry for
him, cause *he* 'ave got summat to mek him
down in the dumps.'

Swish, swish, swish, went the blade of Urbane's
scythe again. The shepherd-harvester was once
more in full swing with his work ; and to make
up for lost time—and no doubt refreshed with
the good meal which he had consumed—he
made some tremendous sweeps with his blade,
and brought down the straws as if they had
been silken threads.

Truly Urbane was 'not a perticklar man';
neither was he an awkward man. He was,
in fact, the handiest man on the Comyn Farm.
Nothing ever came amiss to him. He could
even idle for a few minutes and yet look
comfortable.

'I ought to be sadly mysel' to-day,' he
said, looking round with a smile. 'All my
lambs 'ave just gone to the saleyard. They
were as bonnie a lot as I've ever lambed. But
I inna sad above much. It dunna suit my
constitution, an', o' course, losing a flock o'
lambs inna like losing your very own darlin'
ewe, as Shepherd Armos did.'

With this he bent to the scythe again—
a feature of the landscape; in harmony with
it, a part of it; and I left him singing a
snatch of an old harvest ballad.

The
Leafy
Coombe
THE range of hills in the north-
ward walled in the Red House
Farm, cooming it up as though
it were a tender offspring, and must be sheltered
from the wind.

The red-peaked building was already shaded from the sun. At a distance the peaks only were visible—red cones peeping out from a mass of varied greens. It was as though the house, like a sensitive maid, was not altogether pleased with its appearance, and therefore hid what beauty it had in the depth of green-wood.

It was entirely enveloped in leaves. Trees grew right over its roof. It was in vain, from the outside, to try and see the form of architecture in which the house was built. Only from the farmyard itself could this be seen. Looking at the fabric from the outside was like looking through a trellis work ; here and there only could be seen a picturesque bit of the building.

All human life seemed dead there, as I viewed the farm from the stile which marked the boundary and separated the Comyn Farm from the Red House. Not a living thing in the shape of man, woman or child could be seen in all the wide northward expanse, and yet the oats in the adjoining home close were ripe for cutting.

'QUIETUDE IS THE CHARACTERISTIC OF THE RED HOUSE FARM.'

Quietude is the characteristic of the Red
House Farm. At no hour of the day and
at no season of the year can it be said to be
lively. Occasionally the voice of the farmer
can be heard in the land, complaining, in loud
tones, of the 'contrary seasons,' and of the
ruination they are bringing him to. But these
are only like far-off echoes, spoken from the
belt of high land into which they die, and all
is silence again.

❋ ❋ ❋

The
Farm of
Nature

THAT farm is like the poor
relation of the Comyn Farm
Only the smallest portion of
it is cultivated. Nowhere are seen the evi-
dences of wealth, enterprise and activity that
are observable in the farm over which Urbane
Holt is shepherd.

For upwards of a decade it has worn the
garments of indigence, and now, as the years
go forward, it seems to grow more and more
poverty-stricken. The hedges are broken, the
trees are untrimmed, the claps of the gates are,
in some instances, pulled off. The few cattle
there are on the pastures move slowly about,

as melancholy as the farm itself, as the farmer and the shepherd.

But poverty is picturesque; so there are more signs of natural attraction on the Red House than on the Comyn Farm. The latter is too spick and span. Nature is put to school there. She is not permitted to have her own way, to grow as she pleases, to do just as she likes. There she is in the position of the modern young maid, who is chaperoned daily and nightly, and writhes under the infliction.

At the Red House Farm she is never schooled. She is allowed, like a rosy, healthful child, to run where she listeth. Her hedges are as she grows them. Her trees are her own trees—they are not trimmed to resemble as much as possible the trees of a Noah's Ark.

True, she sometimes runs a little wild, as even Nature will, when left entirely to herself, but her very wildness has a fascination far more attractive than the tameness of a schooled being. And the lethargy of the Red House is all in her favour. She loves its silence, and its manless fields and meadows.

The
Silent
Land-
scape
WHEN I left the boundary stile and walked down the ash-strewn pathway I could hear no sound but the proud cooing of the pert fantails upon the peaks.   Neither could I see a man.   There was the rickyard on the south of the building, paled off from the home close with iron hurdles, looking bright and warm and comfortable as the sun gleamed down upon it and the two yet unthatched ricks ; but there was no human soul there.   The only occupants of the floor of the rickyard just then were nine grey geese and a gander being fattened for the Michaelmas feast.

Sometimes I had found Amos upon the top rung of a ladder thatching a rick, for he was a 'clever hand at thatching, and had won prizes for it at the agricultural shows.   But he was not there now.

As I turned the corner of the black pathway and looked over the privet hedge for a sight of the pyramidal cap of the shepherd, the absence of his familiar figure was a disappointment to me, for in lonely and sequestered regions it is always pleasant to see a well-known face smiling at you, and to hear a well-known voice wishing you 'good-morrow.'

Just as I was wondering whether Amos Oats was sheep-washing in the shallows of the river in the Rungells Meadow, or completing his shearing in the fold behind the farmhouse, a strange, hovering, half-musical sort of noise came to my ears, like the buzzing of a beetle in the gloaming.

I listened, and to me the sound seemed to come from the home close, just by the place where I stood—a thick hedge only dividing us —and appeared to rise from the ground.

There were curious stories in circulation among the farm hands relating to that neigh-bourhood. One was that every now and then the wych-elm on that farm—somewhat further towards the northern hills than where I now was—opened its trunk in the day-time, and that a young maid, instead of an old woman, sat in the hollow and sang songs to the sweetest tunes 'as ever was.'

Rural Ballad NOW the voice that I heard issuing from the hedge bottom, but a short way from where I stood, could not be the voice of the fairy of the wych-elm, simply because there was no wych-elm at that spot, and the sound was bass instead of soprano. I was therefore more interested than fearful, and more delighted than either, when, as I drew softly nearer, the sound shaped itself into words which I well knew as composing a Warwickshire rural ballad of much popularity. It was Shepherd Oats singing 'Lobb's Courtship.'

> As Lobb among his cows one day
> Was filling of their cribs with hay ;
> As he the hay to the cribs did carry,
> It came into his head to marry.

The singer stopped for a moment just then, and I peeped through a gap in the hedge. There was Amos Oats, the shepherd of the Red House Farm, the melancholy man as he was considered, bending down close to the ground, with a fleecy ewe between his legs, clipping its coat off !

He had just taken the forelock off the ewe, and was half singing and half murmuring the ballad, in his deep, rugged voice, as he proceeded with his work, halting now and again when the shears did not act so well as they should have done.

Says he, 'There's little, merry Nell,
I think I like her very well,
Though perhaps at me she'll scoff,
Besides—she lives a long way off.

'When roads are good and weather fine
I'll go and see her—when I've time.'
He mused awhile and judged it better
The courtship to begin by letter.

'Hold still, my lass!' he said to the ewe. It was her first shearing, and though, on the whole, she bore it pretty patiently—lying like a dead thing more than a live one—she at times kicked out vigorously when the point of the shears happened to prick her. With these slight pauses Amos continued his singing.

Then he a bit of paper found,
'Twas neither long, nor square, nor round;
It was the best that he could find,
So on it thus he wrote his mind:

'Cum, cum!' his voice sounded out again between the singing, 'thee knowest I wunna hurt thee. Thou wert my favourite eanling out on all the lambs, an' I wunna hurt a hair on thy pretty head. Be easy, lass!'

> 'Dear Nellie, I make bold to send
> To thee my love, and am your friend,
> If you can like a country man
> I'll come and see you when I can.'

> Then he in haste this letter sent,
> Also two apples did present,
> Which Nell received and read the letter,
> But she liked the apples better.

He paused awhile to take breath and to straighten his back somewhat, for he was by no means a young or strong man, and sheep-shearing—as those know who have had experience of it—is a hot and back-aching branch of pastoral work.

Wiping his top lip with the back of his hand which held the shears, he went on again.

> When read she in the fire threw it,
> And never sent an answer to it,
> Spring drew on and cuckoo sang,
> The roads were good, the days were long.

The cows were all turned out to grass,
And Lobb set off to see his lass.

'Easy, easy, my darlin',' he said to the ewe.
'You be a'most over it now.'

He oiled his shoes and combed his hair,
Like one a-going to a fair.

His stick was bended like a bow,
His handkerchief it made a show,
His hat stood like the pot-lid round,
His coat was of the fustian browned.
And so he went, and Nell he found.

'A clip or two more, my pet, and then you
are finished and so is my song, which I hope
'ave pleased ye, being as this be the first time as
I've trolled it sin my poor gel cum to her ending, worse luck for her, an' me, an' all on us.'

'Dear Nellie, how dost do?' said he,
'Oh! will you come along of me
O'er yonder close to yonder stile?'
'Indeed,' says Nell, 'I can't awhile.'
So Nell steps in and shuts the door,
And Lobb shogged off and said no more.

Amos
Oats.
Shep-
berd

THE singing then ceased. It was the strangest thing I ever heard just at that point, where the only musical effects usually heard were the screaming of the geese when frightened by some chance intruder, or the bleating of the store sheep.

The tune was a slow, catchy one, and as sung by the shepherd, with his head sometimes elevated, at other times muffled in the wool of the shearing ewe, it had a sort of hovering, swinging and floating motion, most peculiar to the senses and quite fascinating to the ear that heard it.

And could this engaging singer, this pastoral songster, who by his quaint and rugged expression of a rural story would hold an accomplished singer interested; could this be Shepherd Oats, the wrinkled, elderly rustic, whose form was like the bent and gnarled codlin tree in the orchard of the Red House? Could this indeed be the melancholy man of whom I had seen and heard so much?

I moved from the bush where I had been

standing and came to a gap in the hedge,
fenced in by a wooden hurdle, and looked
over.

Yes, it was Amos Oats. He had just
released the ewe, who ran bounding over the
close, looking particularly foolish without her
coat, and wondering what on earth made her
feel so light. The shepherd rose from his
knees and straightened out his long, lean
shanks, and looked after the ewe with a
smile breaking over his rugged, weather-worn
features. He looked like a man just rising
from his native bed. His legs were enveloped
in sheep's wool almost up to his knees.

He turned and saw me leaning on the elm-
wood hurdle.

'Her canna mek it out,' he said, a glance
of kindly recognition darting through his
slit-like eyes, as he pulled his peaked cap
closer over them to shade them from the sun.
'Her's bin laid up, and so her's all lag wi'
the shearing. Her's the last on my lot, and
not being dusty like, I warn't in a hurry to
tek her coat off.'

The ewe ran with a gallop round the close,

jumping up high in the air now and then in a state of much perplexity, bleating as she went.

'Em do cut some queer capers at times—unaccountable queer. This un seems more dubersome and illconvenient than reg'lar. But she'll raggle on. Her 'ull get used to it before blindman's-buff.'

'Perhaps the ewe wanted a continuation of your song, Amos?' I suggested. 'I was quite interested in it.'

The shepherd's face expanded into what was meant for a smile, but the moment afterwards all the wrinkles went back into their old places, and the old tired-and-sick-of-life aspect came over the entire countenance. It was as if my allusion to his song brought Shepherd Oats back again to his daily life and to painful memories, from which, for the moment, his singing had lifted him.

'I yent much at songsterin' now,' he said sadly. 'I'm tisiky here, you know,' tapping his lungs, 'an' hanna got the wind as I wunst had. I dunno what made me trip it out this morning, for I hanna trolled it now for ten

year or thereabouts. 'Twere the unaccountable fine weather, a-believe.'

He bent down and gathered up the wool
he had clipped from his favourite ewe. I
believe it was to hide a tear, for as I followed
his action, the sun slanted into the corner of
his eye and seemed to light something which
stood there, until it gleamed like a little
round gem of living fire.

Shepherd Oats there and then assumed his
old form again—a tired, worn, wrinkled old
man, with a melancholy aspect from top to
toe. Even his legs seemed singularly shrunken
and quite out of sorts with the world, and yet,
as far as possible, willing to carry out the duty
expected from them.

He nodded towards the shorn lamb who
was now quietly browsing on the grass.

'Her'll sune forget as her's lost her top-
coat,' he said with another expansion of his
visage which was meant for another smile.

Then he picked up the ewe's coat, and rolled
it into the form of a good-sized rug. This
he placed under his arm, and in the other
hand carried his shears. A moment after-

wards he sidled off like a man utterly bone
weary, nodding his pyramidal cap to me by
way of farewell.

He was a mournful picture—the reverse
side of the rural medal to the cheerful
shepherd of the Comyn Farm. Poor Amos!
But he was quite in keeping with his sur-
roundings. He was part of the picturesque
scene ; an actor in it ; inseparable from it.
Dark as the hills frowned upon the coombe
in winter—so was he.

Rural Merrymakings

Rural Merrymakings

How often have I blessed the coming day,
When toil remitting lent its turn to play,
And all the village train from labour free
Led up their sports beneath the spreading tree.
Goldsmith.

Many a youth and many a maid
Dancing in the chequer'd shade.
Milton.

The Customs of the Country
IN pictures of country life there are few more interesting than those illustrative of rustic pleasures. These sports at the village alehouse, on the village green, or in the rickyard of a farmhouse are so truly delightful and so eminently English that we would not willingly let one of them die.

On the whole there is more Conservatism than Radicalism in an Englishman's nature. All of us in one way or in another are antiquaries; and none would like to see the merrymakings of the village submerged by the waters of modern civilisation.

The village is a town undeveloped. There are no streets, but there are places that answer to the streets in towns. Every rood of land almost has a name. In the neighbourhood of the Red House Farm, from east to west, from north to south, there is a variety of names which sound foreign or quaint to the ear of the city dweller.

In the place from which I write, we have such patronymics as 'The Home Close,' 'Innidge Meadow,' 'The Gravel-Pit Farm,' 'The Ham,' 'Raven's Close,' 'The Hill Field,' 'Nabbs' Lammas Closes,' 'The Shell Leys,' and 'The Bancroft.' Even as roods and perches are baptised, so almost every class of villager has a periodic merrymaking.

The Earth-stoppers   A CLASS of country folk very little known outside its own orbit is the class called earth-stoppers.   As examples of natural history

these men are interesting. They are known
better to the vulpine than to the human race.
Foxes consider them their bitterest enemies,
for they prevent them from reaching their
earths when the hounds are after them in
full cry.

They erect barricades in front of Mr Fox's
house, so that he cannot enter when hard
pressed. Yet the earthstoppers are merry
fellows and make merry as well as the rest.
It is the custom in Warwickshire to give
these useful servants of the hunt a jolly rous-
ing every year—generally in May. The chair
is taken by one of the principal landowners
or by a fox-hunting farmer. When the
latter can be persuaded to perform the
function, the merrymaking is all the more
cordial, for the fox-hunting farmer of Warwickshire is a jovial soul, full of heart and
merriment.

⚜ ⚜ ⚜

In the
· Red
Lion ·
T the sign of the 'Red Lion,'
upon an evening in May or
June, the earthstoppers meet

one another, and it is worth all the merrymaking in the world to be with them. They
sidle and shamble up to the tavern, one by
one, in that half-ashamed manner peculiar to
rustics when asked to eat or to drink at
another's expense.

When they get together in the snug parlour
of 'The Lion,' they are all right. Indeed
they would be all right if they walked to
the place of merrymaking in a body. It is
the walking up in ones and twos, and the
consciousness that they are being 'twigged'
by the onlookers that causes their awkward-
ness. And, after all, your severe critic is
the yokel who does not stand upon refine-
ment, but speaks his words just as ''em
cum.'

Whether or not his shafts of bucolic wit
penetrate the agricultural cranium can be
decided only by the kind of smile with
which the rustic receives them. If his face
becomes full of puckers he is pleased, for
the wit has but just touched him; if only
a frigid expansion of the lips is observable,
the shaft has penetrated and it hurts.

Like other occupants of villages, the earth-stopper 'inna fit for a tune' until he has reached the bottom of his third quart pot. Then the difficulty is to restrain him from favouring the company overmuch. His desire to sing is equalled by his desire to speak, 'if so be as the company's agreeable.'

After he has sung 'When Bonnie Blue Cap left the Pack'—a very pathetic canine ballad, describing the going away of Blue Cap, the favourite bitch—he will launch out eloquently upon the merits of the pack, somewhat in this style, it may be, 'A lot o' nice dogs, sir, these; a very 'andsume dog, sir, that black and white bitch! A perfect picture, sir, that bay dog with a mixed chocolate-coloured 'edd!! I like these 'unting dogs, with long, crooked fore—and short hind—legs, with a very large web foot. 'Elps 'em to get through the dirt, and elbows well out. Enables 'em to skip nimbly over the briars in the 'oods. I likes 'em, too, with a thin, smooth tail.'

The
Earth-
stop-
pers'
Char-
acter-
istics

WITH all their faults of diction, dress and style, however, the earthstoppers are a merry set of fellows. You should be standing outside the 'Red Lion' when they are having their annual merrymaking. The little panes in the quaint windows of the inn seem ready to come clattering from their frames.

You see, the yokel has a big foot and a large hand. When he brings the one down on the table and the other on the floor, it is as if the man had a talent for turning houses inside out.

Perhaps, however, one of the strongest characteristics of the earthstopper, or, indeed, of any villager, is his regard for the Master of the Pack, or the person who does him a good turn. There are people who underrate the sympathies of Strephon, and think that because he is not 'eddicated,' and is a little rough in his dress, and sometimes gives olfactory proof of his occupation, he is 'an ignorant boor' without feelings.

Never was opinion more erroneous ; never was the superior education of cities more at fault. Your rustic may be ignorant of book learning—'larning,' he calls it ; he may be, and very likely is, provokingly dense and amusingly thick-skinned ; but when he is attached to anyone, no Corsican can hate so well as the 'ignorant boor' can love.

From 1854 to 1862, Mr John Baker, a sportsman well known in the Midlands, was Master of the North Warwickshire Foxhounds. During his tenure he was stricken down with a severe illness for several months. His well-to-do friends were deeply concerned ; his earth-stoppers were inconsolable.

❦ ❦ ❦

The Rustic's Songstering. NOW the average yokel is a creature without much music in his soul ; at the same time he is not necessarily fit only for 'treasons, stratagems and spoils.' With a skinful of liquor he can troll an ancient ditty, but in his sober moments he 'hanna much gift for songstering.'

Devotion, however, will inspire men to the accomplishment of designs which 'they hanna

bin used to,' and it did in the case under notice.
When the Master, released from the jaws of
Death, made his appearance in the hunting field,
the earthstoppers welcomed him with a song,
'composed expressly for the occasion.' It was
set to the tune of, 'Oh! Willie, We have missed
You,' and was as follows,—

O, Master, is it you, sir, safe arrived at home?
They did not tell us true, sir; they said you would not
    come.
We heard you at the door, and it made us all rejoice,
As we knew your welcome footfall, and your dear, familiar
    voice
Like music in our ears as we through woodlands roam;
O, Master, we have missed you! welcome to our home.

We've longed to see you daily, but this day most of all,
Old Saucebox looked so gaily, and Ringwood heard you
    call;
The young hounds were in high glee as they heard your
    footsteps pass,
Such whimpering was heard aloud, but now there's peace
    at last;
We patiently did wait, yet thought you would not come,
O, Master, we have missed you! welcome to our home.

The days were long without you, the field seemed dull
    and drear,
Inquiring all about you and when you would be here;

We were days in anxious doubt when you were far away,
But in the black and stormy clouds there's oft a cheering
ray ;
So we all rejoiced again when we heard that you had
come,
O, Master, we have missed you ! welcome to our home.

This is not bad for the 'uneddicated' peasant.
It shows that his heart is in the right place, if
his head is not crammed ' wi' larning.'

In the 'George and Dragon' OTHER country folk who each
year enjoy a merrymaking are
the game-preservers and beaters·
To be at a gathering of these people is to
become acquainted with some glimpses of
natural history undreamt of in the philosophy
of city dwellers.

As an English merrymaking is synonymous
with feeding, so the merrymaking of game-
preservers and covert-beaters is made round
the mahogany in the best room at the 'George
and Dragon.' Those only who have been in
the best room of 'The George' can compre-
hend the comfort conveyed in the line,—

'Shall I not take mine ease in mine inn ? '

Newly-polished seats, without a speck of
dust upon them; a blackened mantelshelf
adorned at each end with a quart pot of spills;
a table without a beer stain, but decorated
at the four corners with cigar-ash dishes; a
gas-bracket bedizened with a frill - work of
coloured papers; sparkling glasses of the best
October brews; an odour of something savoury
from the kitchen; to crown all, the intermittent presence of as fine and cheerful a
hostess as can be found in Warwickshire
—these are a few, a very few, of the
delights of the best room in the 'George
and Dragon.'

The
Furry
Bird's
Nester
AND they are fully appreciated
by the merrymaking game-
preservers and covert-beaters,
who squeeze every drop of pleasure out of the
meeting. As I have hinted, however, there
are one or two items in the merriment which
are more interesting than roystering.

These are dealt with before the cups pass

and repass, are filled and are emptied. In truth
it is better so; for if any serious business were
treated of when the rustics are 'in their cups,'
not a word of it would they remember when
reason and sleep had sobered them.

Among the preservers and beaters generally
are several boys, or creatures between the boy
and the youth. Theirs is a tender age and
one peculiarly apt to imbibe knowledge. Now
before the effects of the merrymaking cloud
the brains of these village goslings, the gamekeeper or bailiff, or some other worthy who
happens to sit or stand in authority at the
mahogany, delivers 'a bit o' speech' for the
benefit and edification of these younger hands.

You should see the faces of the rustic rascals
when the speechifying begins. Strephon in
miniature may be as dense and ignorant as
Strephon in full growth; but he in miniature
has more humour.

'Now the preaching's goin' fur to begin,'
whispers one to another, and their already
broad faces expand like balloons being filled
with gas. By-and-by, however, their cheeks
contract to their original shape, for the person

who is on 'his stumps' is 'preaching' something which interests them. It is really of interest (or should be) to all lovers of natural history, whether they be merrymaking or not.

What the speechifier is saying may be reduced to the following language,—

'You young 'uns are fond o' bird's nesting, now inna you? Well, some day belike you'll come along o' a partridge's nest wi' eggs in it. If you do, all as I say to you is this, don't you be anxious to see the hen lay her eggs. You leave her to lay 'em whenever she has a mind so to do. She'll tak' pretty good care to lay 'em at the right time.

'Now what am I telling you this for? Why, so as you wunna let that other bird's nester (a worser one than any o' you are) know where that nest be. I mean the weasel, you know. That's a cunnin' chap, that is. If you once mak' a pathway through yon grass, the weasel 'ull foller it, find the nest, an' suck the eggs as soon as the partridge 'as laid 'em. Belike he'll collar the poor dame herself if he can. An' you see you canna catch a weasel asleep; what's more, you canna prosecute him under

Act o' Parliament for breaking the game laws.'

'The young uns,' the tail of the game-preservers and covert-beaters, listen with faces as sober as judges. His 'speechifying' sounds very much like something they, being country boys, have heard before ; but they give their attention to it as if it were as brand new as the clean polish upon their own faces—put on expressly for the merrymaking. They could probably tell the land-agent—who is speaking —more bird and weasel-lore than he could imagine ; but they hold their peace and listen.

The Decay of Rustic Pleasures

MERRYMAKINGS like these, in the snug taprooms of village inns, are characteristic of English country life, which the novelist and painter will do well not to forget. They are so quaint, so cheering, and not devoid of the picturesque. But there are out-door rejoicings yet in existence—the remnant of a merrymaking race —which should not go unremembered.

In Warwickshire there used to be many pretty and quaint forms of outdoor merry-making, which, alas! are now more honoured in the breach than in the observance. The town has crawled nearer and nearer to the village; what is known as 'modern civilisation' has descended upon the hamlet nestling among the woodlands; and the sweeping changes have conspired in many places to run much of the quaint and picturesque out of existence.

Still, in the south part of Shakespeare's shire, the searcher after old English customs can find a remnant of them left. For one thing, rural Warwickshire is secluded, and change cannot so easily penetrate through barricades of greenwood. Besides, the rustics of the classic shire are long-lived, and customs, especially home customs, are handed down from parents to children, in the same way as the great ones of the city hand down their family heirlooms.

The
Roasted
Crabs   I MYSELF have noticed with
pleasure that one old Warwickshire home custom, alluded to
by Shakespeare, still survives. This is the
roasting of the crab. In the time of the
poet this was a jovial winter dish. Crabs
were roasted and then put into a spacious
bowl of spiced ale.

Speaking of this, Shakespeare says,—

> When roasted crabs hiss in the bowl
> Then nightly sings the staring owl.

In many cottages the crab is still roasted.
Sometimes it is plunged into a bowl of hot
spiced ale; at other times into a dish of
stewed sago.

The
May
Day
Merry-
making   ONE of the most pretty and
popular merrymakings still observed in rural Warwickshire
is the May Day festival. In
the early years of the present century, indeed,

May Day was a high day and holiday in
many of the leading towns. It was one of
the principal holidays of the year, but since
the consecration of St Lubbock, the May
Day merrymaking has continued to be chiefly
observed in villages.

Perhaps it has lost none of its charms by
retreating from the towns. In the latter, the
festival assumed a circus-like glamour, not so
innocent nor so pleasant as the smaller and
less tawdry merrymaking on the village green.
Therefore its decline and discontinuance in
places where 'men most do congregate' is
not so much to be regretted as it would be
if it were to decline in those pleasant nooks
'far from the madding crowd.'

In a little circle round Stratford-on-Avon
the observance of the May Day *fête* is obeyed
with rigid regularity. The village children
of Charlecote, Bidford, Grafton, Kineton,
and other adjacent places, would open their
bright, round eyes and wonder if they
were told there was to be no maypole
and no May Day feast and pleasure. In
one of his simplest and prettiest poems

THE RED AND FALLOW DEER OF CHARLECOTE.

By permission of Messrs Eyre & Spottiswoode.

Lord Tennyson has immortalised the May Queen :—

'You must wake and call me early, call me early, mother dear,
To-morrow will be the happiest time of all the glad New Year ;
Of all the glad New Year, mother, the maddest, merriest day,
For I'm to be Queen of the May, mother, I'm to be Queen of the May.'

The late Poet Laureate would seem to have been well acquainted with Warwickshire lore. In that shire of romance, history and poetry, the election of the May Queen is decided upon overnight, just as in the Laureate's ballad. The thoughts occupying the mind of the chosen one, from the time of her election to her coronation, may be better imagined than described.

No wonder Tennyson should depict *his* Queen enjoining her mother to wake her early. I have no doubt that many a Warwickshire lass from time immemorial has done the same.

At Charlecote and the neighbouring villages and hamlets, the May Day merrymaking is a

M

delightful one for the children. For 'children of larger growth'—in this case meaning the vicar, his wife, his curate, his curate's wife (if he has one) and their well-to-do friends—this merrymaking has certain attractions. There are, happily, people who can always extract pleasure out of making other people happy; and this class generally comprises the vicar of the parish and his fellow workers. All, or much, at any rate, depends upon the weather. If it is fine, the merrymaking is glorious; if it is wet—why, the merrymaking is then considerably damped.

In Warwickshire—strictly adhering to time-honoured usages—the people of the villages hold their May festival on 'Old May Day'—the 12th of the month. On the day before, the village green is invaded by an army of small merrymakers and a few older ones. They bring whatever flowers they can, and straightway proceed to garland, festoon and raise the maypole.

On the morrow they are as gay as the maypole—if the weather is fine—round which they dance. Indeed, there is no prettier or more touching scene in English pastoral life than the merrymaking of the children on May Day in that classic county which the poets have called 'Leafy Warwickshire.'

FINIS

Colston & Coy., Limited, Printers, Edinburgh.